Paperback Thriller

Paperback Thriller

Lynn Meyer

Random House: New York

For David

Quid rides? Mutato nomine, de te fabula narratur.

—Horace

Paperback Thriller

Part One

One

What is normal?

After three days of papers, discussions, study groups, cocktail parties, and formal banquets, the question had not been answered. But I had decided it was definitely not normal to spend all that time in meetings, redefining, revaluating, reconsidering, from the psychiatric, sociological, and anthropological points of view the parameters of normality. Parameters! They just adore words like that. They stand up there and say "parameters" or "sociometric" or some such thing, and the meaning of the word is lost in the other meaning, that exchange of winks that we're professional, we're special, we're just too damned wonderful . . . Secret passwords to the clubhouse they've built high up in the tree. And no sense of humor. I mean, how can a man named Arnold Moffat deliver a paper called "The Kurdish Way"? Nobody smiled, nobody exchanged little glances. All very straight and earnest. Which is not what I'd like to think is normal. No, ma'am, no, thank you.

I had come to Philadelphia because John was coming. And he was there because I was there. As a matter of fact, it would not be surprising if most of the members of the conference were there for the same reasons that we were, sitting through the sessions as a way of justifying to their wives or husbands, the Internal Revenue Service, and their tight puritan souls the three-day spree. For all I know, the minute the meetings ended, they were all doing what John and I were doing, tearing out of there and upstairs to the real business of the conference, and fucking their brains out.

John and I have this nice civilized arrangement. We couldn't stand each other on any permanent basis. He is attractive, and witty, and smart, and great fun, but he is an incurable chauvinist pig. He couldn't stand living with me, and I couldn't stand his not being able to stand it. But for what the old madams used to call short-time, we suit each other. Oh, I imagine that if I wanted to devote my life to it, I could reform him. But what would Arlene do, back in Denver? One can't go around rehabilitating everyone. Arlene is his wife—whom he loves because she is stable and steady and good at cooking and scrubbing and praising. Listen, I'm not knocking it. Everybody needs a wife like that, men and women both. It's just that slavery was abolished a long time ago.

For the short haul, though, John is great fun. We sat through meetings together with cue words. If anyone said "ethnocentric" or "consensual validation" or whatever we'd picked out the night before, that would be our cue to get up, leave, and go upstairs. It helped us get through some of the more pedestrian presentations.

A lot of food, a lot of booze, a lot of sex, and then, just before all our spirits began to wilt, and some of us came down with bride's disease, the conference ended. And I was on my way back to Cambridge. I was in the airport. I checked my bag through, and asked the ticket agent when the plane would be boarding.

"About twenty minutes," she said, and flashed a baboon grin at me. The baboons really do grin that way. It is a submissive gesture and a plea that the other baboon will not hit. I wasn't going to hit her. I smiled back. And her smile changed, became almost real. It must be a hell of a strain to have to smile all the time as a part of the job. To have to smile to people who never return the gesture. It is still submission. Just as wearing those cute costumes that actually are a kind of livery. John, Arlene, the ticket agent . . . It's all around, flying in thick chunks through the bad air. And one can't do everything, can one?

With twenty minutes to kill, I thought I'd go get a cup of coffee, but the choice was between one of those restaurants where the service is fantastically slow just because there are tablecloths, or a snack bar. I walked toward the snack bar, walked up to the entrance, and then turned away. The smell of old fat was overpowering. They must fry galoshes in that fat. Not even the poor cows they grind up and fry could account for that smell. I could tell you now that I'm a vegetarian, but let's just leave it at that. I won't go into the reasons. If you don't understand them, there's not much I can say; and if you do, there's no need for me to say anything. It all goes back to a duckling I had when I was a kid. It grew up to be a duck, and then we killed it and cooked it. And I wouldn't eat it. Couldn't. From that, it was all obvious and logical. Logic, however, as the conference proved, is not at all normal. Damned rare, in fact.

Anyway, bowled back from the snack bar—named, of course, after one of the great chefs—I went over to the newsstand. I thought I might pick up a paperback to read on the plane, or just to hold in case I felt like reading. Or to pretend to read if I needed to cut off the stupid conversation of some believer in the Perfect Master or an advocate of Scientology. The world is full of ancient mariners, and they're all out of their minds, and they stop about one in three—Coleridge had the odds right, I think. But the chances are better (or worse) in public conveyances. So it's good to have a book. I can take care of lechers. The trick is to gross them out. "Skip the talk, Mac. Show me your cock," and the guy will get up and walk away, the way women used to have to do. And if he does hang in there and unzip—which has never happened to me—you just shake your head, say it's too small, and pick up your knitting. Or your book.

I guess I wanted the book in case I got thoughtful. These transitions can be tough, and people find themselves asking difficult questions. I was tired enough to be vulnerable, and I didn't want to have to face the kind of question that might arise: Can a thirty-five-year-old, divorced, vegetarian, feminist psychiatrist with two lovers and an Angora cat find happiness and fulfillment? Better to read a not too demanding book, get through the flight, and leave that sort of doubt to a time when the energy level is higher.

In the newsstand, there were racks and racks of those gaudy covers, all of them flashing out their sad promises of achievement and of love. That's what all those hieroglyphs really stand for. All you have to do is translate those heaving bosoms and flaming guns to sex and violence, and then convert those into what people really want. Adventure is to achievement as sex is to love, right? But you can understand how the trick works and still enjoy watching it if it's done well enough. You can't switch your mind to *off,* but you can put it in *idle.*

Figure all those covers as the doodles and drawings of a single person, and the diagnosis is pretty clear: an anal-compulsive, sado-masochistic paranoid, probably retarded. Still, paranoia can be interesting. The rage for order that violently unifies all occurrences tempts

5

even the most sophisticated reader. Even me. I enjoy spies and private eyes as much as anyone, and it is soothing to imagine a world in which they operate, proving the innocence of the good, and destroying the wicked, saving the virtue of the whole world or a small piece of it.

My attention caught at a cover that showed a bare breast with a revolver and a flower tattooed just above the nipple. The purity of its foolishness was refreshing. I was also pleased with the author's name. There just couldn't be a real person called Greg Pitman. A pseudonym, then, and for a non-book to have a non-person as its author was intricate enough to please me. *Do Not Go Gentle*—a quote from Dylan Thomas, yet!

I picked it up and looked at the back, reading the publisher's pitch. The blurb announced, with a wit that may even have been intentional: "Greg Pitman's speed and pace are awesome . . . a real whiz!" The endorser, Jack Towne, was not a name I'd heard of. Maybe the publisher made him up, too. I hoped so.

For such dumb reasons, then, I bought the book, exchanged the baboon smiles with the cashier, and walked down the long corridor toward the plane. I went through the search, which is a nuisance. I know, I know. Better to have my bag opened than to have some mad bomber get on the plane with me. And I'm sure the security people are utterly bored, their curiosity having been entirely extinguished in the first couple of hours on the job. They are professionals, like me, and they look into briefcases and handbags the way we look into psyches. Both jobs are supposed to protect society by looking for explosive devices. The psychological explosives are just as dangerous. And yet there is a kind of soiling, not so much by the fingers of the guards as they rummaged through my Gucci carryall as by the idea of menace. It's like the smell of disinfectant in hospitals that always makes me think of the germs the disinfectants are supposed to kill. Give them a couple of thousand years and the germs will learn to smell of disinfectant.

A couple of thousand years? Do we have that much to give? Going toward a plane, my thoughts always turn dark. And the rest of the world helps the darkness along. It searches your bag, it provides you with a book about violence and death—really sets you up, right? It's what comes of slaughtering gentle creatures, cows and lambs and silly chickens and cuddly ducks . . . But I promised I wouldn't get into that.

Feeling skittish, though, for whatever combination of rational and irrational causes, I sat down in one of those modules, a chair connected to a table which was in turn connected to a chair. It was an ugly piece of furniture, uncomfortable, grotesque . . . The only possible reason for it was that it's just too damned cumbersome to steal. But it looked as though the squared chunks were manacled together. An airport full of potential killers, and the furniture looked like a bunch of fugitives. Fatigue, of course, on my part, but you'd think they would account for that. Most of the people in airports are tired. All of them are open to the same kinds of dark thoughts. Who needs it? I'd had a good time, for God's sake! What about the people who had come away from a bummer?

I sat there, building these intellectual constructions, letting my mind wander. In front of me there was a big picture window, and because it was dark outside, the window reflected back, became a sullied mirror in which passengers, crew, ticket agents, porters, stewardesses all floated like so many soiled ghosts of themselves. I looked at my own reflection, inspecting my own ghost.

Perhaps I should describe myself. Tall, fair, thin. On a good day, willowy; on a less good day, a stick. I correspond to the mannequin ideal, which makes it easy to buy clothes. Great legs but not much in the front. I'm old enough so that I'm used to my body by now, but when I was a kid, I envied the huge front of Jane Russell. And I was too tall. I was the tallest girl in the eighth grade, and I freckled in the summer. Hated it. But after a weekend with John, I felt pretty good about myself. Or maybe I was just too tired to be critical. Either way, I looked interesting in that dark glass, the lights of the airport shining through in places to make the ghostliness even stranger. As if we were all sitting there waiting to be turned into constellations, the way the Greek heroes used to do. My constellation would be a shambles. Me, John, Martin, and the cat, all jumbled up. And maybe, with one second magnitude star, Roger, my ex-husband. Not a bad man, Roger, but the victim of an incomplete revolution. Like me. Like all of us.

Lately I have thought of him with less anger and more regret, but that is probably a sign that I've let him go at last. Anger is what you feel when there is still a future. Regret is for the past. It was a choice between his life and mine, and I chose for myself. Which is what feminism and liberation is all about. It is necessary and right, but nobody ever said it was fun.

With that kind of thinking bubbling up from the subconscious water table, I pulled out the paperback and was just opening it when the ticket agent appeared at the little desk to announce that the plane would be boarding momentarily. She invited the passengers to present their tickets. I got in line behind two sailors. They were going back to their base from a weekend leave. Young, mindlessly attractive, they looked haggard from the strenuousness of their entertainments. The poor dears. I wondered whether they'd had as good a time as I'd had, and hoped so, until one of them laughed, a silly high whinny. Men ought to learn to keep their stupid mouths closed. I changed my mind, hoped he'd had a terrible time, hoped that neither one had scored and that they had a long tour of sea duty ahead of them. And I caught myself. What difference did the poor bastard's laugh make?

This all sounds incredibly stupid and picky, but it's important. The mood and tone of how it was came out of all these dumb little details. Airports and airplanes are enough to make anyone a little bit crazy, and I was tired, and horny after leaving John, and on edge. I was regretting not having braved the smells of the snack bar to get coffee. I could have had them put it in a container and walked away. I could have carried it to this boarding lounge and it would have been at least warm. I was thinking about that as I handed my ticket to the agent, picked a seat, and then returned to my chain-gang chair to wait for them to open the gate. Finally they did, and we all boarded, and I sat down and started to read. I read all during the takeoff, as if takeoffs were perfectly safe, and up through some bumpy clouds. I put it down because it was boring, and then I picked it up again. And then I found that paragraph in the beginning of Chapter Three. I read it, stopped, went back, and with a different kind of attention, read it again:

Four walls, a desk, a couch, a pair of club chairs, and, along one wall, a row of steel files in expensive powder-blue. What kind of maniac designs powder-blue files? Or buys them? On a shelf on the wall, behind the desk and out of reach of destructive patients, there was a lapis-lazuli horse. On the desk itself, there was an old-fashioned turnip of a pocket watch, hanging on a silver holder, the holder worked in vine leaves and the whole thing covered by a little bell jar. On the wall opposite, there was an etching of a man's head, one of those stylish things to reassure patients that madness could pay. The etching was distorted with herringbone patterns wrenching the jaw one way and the nose another, the pattern slamming back and forth like blows.

Brad Steele did not hurry. There was all the time in the world. He held his flashlight on the etching for a moment, and then addressed the files. He took the picklock from his pocket and with the dexterity of a clever boy manipulated the tool until at last the tumblers tumbled and the lock popped out, open. He drew the drawer of the file toward him. Dr. Pendergast's patients' secrets yawned wide . . .

Brad Steele was a figment of Greg Pitman's imagination. But the watch in the fine-leaved holder, the lapis-lazuli horse, and the Harold Tovish etching were real. I knew they were real because they were all in my office. So were the powder-blue files.

Two

Rape!

No exaggeration. After all, what is rape but the ultimate invasion of privacy. And I found myself prickling with sweat as the adrenalin and the capillaries did their number. Terrific. I was all ready to fight off the attacker, but there was no one to fight. I was sitting there in a plane three and a half miles up in the air, reading about something that had happened . . . When? I checked back to the copyright page. Last year? Figure a year to write the book and get it through the process of publication. So, a year and a half, maybe two years ago. My office, my files, my patients. And some stranger had been rooting around there? Yuck!

With a new kind of attention, fascinated and repelled, I whipped through the rest of the book, hoping and fearing that I might recognize something—or someone—else. But there was nothing else. It was a conventional spy caper, the old battle between the forces of good and the forces of evil, with a dollop of sex and a lacing of violence. Mostly it was a delusionary fantasy about a deep-cover agent, the villain being a fellow who had been planted years before, had led a quiet life in a Middle American city, and then, on signal, resumed his true identity to threaten all of us . . . It was Clark Kent slipping into a phone booth to get out of that nasty electric-blue suit he always wore. Or Batman coming out of the closet. Pure dreamland.

But in that imaginary garden, there was the one real toad. Or turd. My office. Not the office I have at the clinic, but my office at home, where I see patients in the afternoons. And with as much calm and objectivity as I could muster, I tried to consider whether it might not be a coincidence. But to duplicate in a random way such a peculiar combination of objects was just not plausible. No way. But couldn't there be some explanation other than a burglary? One of my patients, perhaps?

The sweat began to dry, and the dryness in my mouth started to melt a little. Here was a reasonable assumption, a way out . . . And I clutched at it. The possibility became a probability. There were hints enough in the names, which were obviously assumed, invented. They were obvious invitations to disbelief. The name of the hero was Brad Steele. In real life there might well be such witless extravagance. I remembered one of my friends at Vassar telling me about a cousin whose name was Ginger Snapp. In art, however, there are restrictions, and jokes are presumed to be intentional. I had to assume that this was a way of hinting, of conspiring with the reader with a small wink and a nervous wave, and to suggest that the book was only fun and games, not to be taken too seriously. And the name of the author, too, was a similar disclaimer. Greg Pitman? The two leading systems of shorthand? Nobody was likely to be named that. (Or, if he was, he would assume another name to appear to be real.)

What I inferred, then, was a pattern in these gestures, one of which was the inclusion of these details from my office. Invitations to be recognized, to be discovered. What other function could the description have served? It did nothing to further the pace or development of the narrative. It did not contribute very much to the tone or mood. The psychiatrist whose files Brad Steele examined never even appeared, himself. So it had to be a game of some kind, one of the games people play—when they are desperate. A pseudonymous author was begging to be recognized, hiding behind the fictitious identity and yet calling out, "Here I am, over here! It's me! It's me!"

The title itself, a line from a Dylan Thomas poem, was the same kind of call to readers, inviting them to understand that the author was a man of some culture, even though he was writing dumb spy novels. Almost certainly, then, it had to be a patient. If only the patient had sent me a copy of the book . . .

But then, that assumed that the patient was reasonable and sane. "Normal"—whatever that means. In which case, the patient would not have been a patient. I wondered which one of them it could be. An interesting question, for in theory a psychiatrist ought to be able to identify a patient by symptoms. At least to winnow out a probable handful. And if it came to that, it would be exactly what I might have to do. But first there was the direct approach, through the publisher. I could call up and ask who the hell Greg Pitman really was.

The seat-belt sign went on and I gave myself up to pure process—the business of landing, taxiing, waiting, deplaning, getting my suitcase, getting a cab. I was tired, but that only made it all the better to be home. A trite thing to say, but it's perfectly true. I remember looking out of the cab window at the Charles and feeling good about the river, about Boston and Cambridge, about belonging to the place and having the place, therefore, belong to me. I even felt good about the recklessness of the driver—which was perfectly standard for Bostonian cabbies. Of course, after he left the main arteries, got into Cambridge, and approached my house, I had to give him instructions and help him find the cul-de-sac off Brattle Street where I live. And once he was reduced to having to take instructions, his driving changed, slowed to a pace that was nearly legal. Which may explain why they all drive so badly when they know the way. It's stored-up frustration, an assertion of independence and competence. Machismo! Which is okay if they don't hit a light stanchion.

True or not, the formulation was reasonable enough to be comforting. Figure something out and you are its master; it can't hurt you. Something like that. I had a theory about the cabbie, and I would live through the cab ride. Just as I had a theory about the author of *Do Not Go Gentle* as a patient of mine. And until the theory collapsed, the book could not threaten me, the cold sweat could not return to clutch me.

We pulled up to the curb at the circular turnaround. I paid and probably tipped too much, and turned toward the house. It is one of those square, wood, probably ugly houses. I can't tell any more. There is a boxy kind of Cambridge house to which, after a while, one becomes accustomed and which one even learns to like. I am fond of mine, as of some weird breed of dog. I keep it up, and the neighborhood is unpretentious but expensive. And so the house survives, getting more valuable every year, able to carry off with some style what another house in another neighborhood could not.

I let myself in through the front door—where can you find those old cut-glass panes in huge oak doors any more?—and stepped into the room that had once been a parlor and was now my consulting room. I dropped my bag, switched on the light, and gathered up the mail that had accumulated during the time I'd been away. Stanley had piled it all on my desk. I flipped through the envelopes. No surprises, and nothing urgent. I put it back down. I looked around, unable to help myself. At the lapis horse, the Tovish etching, the old pocket watch that had belonged to my father. And I took the paperback out of my purse and put it on the desk in the center of the blotter, for tomorrow's attention. Dump it there. Right, and go upstairs to soak for a while in a hot tub and get into bed.

It was eleven in the morning before I was able to think about Greg Pitman again. I had put in three fifty-minute hours at the clinic, and I was on my way back to Cambridge. I was tooling along in my fireman's-red Buick convertible, a scarf around my hair, my pocket Sony in my lap ready to take dictation. I should have been talking about my patients, should at least have been thinking about them. But Greg Pitman had popped back into my head. I'd managed to thrust him aside for most of the morning, had turned my attention to the problems of my poor flock. Now, with a couple of hours to myself, I had practical questions to answer. First of all, why the pseudonym? There are all kinds of reasons for pseudonyms, I had thought only of the psychiatric reason, the wish to be discovered, the put-down come-on. But there were other, more practical reasons. It could be an open secret, like C. Day Lewis's being Nicholas Blake, or John Dickson Carr being Carter Dickson. Or it could be a real secret, a David St. John type who turned out to be E. Howard Hunt. It could be a more difficult thing than I'd figured on. At any rate, it would not hurt to be careful.

When I got back to the house, I made two calls. The first was to Aspen Books in Manhattan. I got a Ms. Gormley in the subsidiary rights department and came on like a film company. I wanted to know about the availability of the film rights to *Do Not Go Gentle*.

"Are you the principal?" Ms. Gormley wanted to know. Some sister, with the Ms. and all, and still she couldn't take anyone seriously who wasn't a man.

"Mr. Harris is in Majorca," I told her. Harris is Sarah pronounced backwards. Majorca is the kind of place some Gormleys still think is fun.

It didn't matter a whole lot. Ms. Gormley didn't know. But she thought that Mr. Druckman of Master Artists Corporation would be able to tell me.

I got Mr. Druckman's phone number. And I asked her, as though I couldn't care less and wanted it only for my Rolodex file, what Mr. Pitman's address and phone number were.

"I'm sorry," she told me. "We don't have that information. Mr. Druckman will be able to help you, I'm sure."

I thanked her and hung up, worried now, because my guess was that she was telling the truth. She hadn't said that she couldn't give out the information—Pitman's address and number—but that she didn't have it. And being the kind of officious bitch I assumed her to be, she would have much preferred to have it and not give it out than not to have it. Assume that there was some seriousness to the pseudonym, some reality to the secret? I had to.

It was a quarter of twelve. I was hungry, but more important, I wanted to think for a little. I went out to the kitchen to fix some fruit and cottage cheese for myself. And tea. On a tray, arranged nicely, paying attention to what I was doing in order to withdraw my attention from the other thing. Just a look away, and there is a degree of freshness to the next glance, a clarity to patterns that were not discernible before. I brought the tray back to my desk and started to eat. I glanced at the phone. I had a sort of rough plan, peculiar but possible. The question was whether or not this Mr. Druckman was likely to be in his office at noon. If he was, then I could be an editor in a Boston publishing house with some interest in Mr. Pitman's work. And if he was not in? The chances were that he would be out having lunch. That could be dangerous, but more amusing. I had another spoonful of cottage cheese, and placed the call, station-to-station. No sense in putting it off, or letting the complications and cautions build up.

In the event, Mr. Druckman was out of the office. "Is there anything I can do?" a female voice asked, not identifying herself.

"When will Mr. Druckman be back?" I asked her.

"Later on this afternoon. Who is calling, please?"

I took a deep breath, and let it rip. "This is Edith Gormley. Of Aspen Books. I'm in subsidiary rights over here. There was a call this morning about *Do Not Go Gentle*. A man in Boston, named Harris. He's going to Majorca tonight. He wants to talk to Greg Pitman, and if that goes well, there might be a deal. But we don't have a phone number for Mr. Pitman. Can you get it for me?"

"One moment, please," the voice said. She left me hanging. Was Druckman really out? Was there a Druckman? Or would she just be checking some file for the phone number. I hadn't asked for the name. Presumably Ms. Gormley knew who the hell Greg Pitman was. But a phone number? They might not guard that with the same

14

caution. Particularly if they smelled money somewhere. I waited, not counting the message units but trying to imagine an office large enough to have so many files that the nameless female could still be looking through them. Or were there other people with whom she would want to confer? Or was she singing the alphabet song to try to remember where P comes. The seconds ticked away on the turnip watch. My hope guttered as my apprehension glowed.

But the woman came back to the phone. "I have it now," she said, and apologized for having taken so long. "I had to look in Mr. Druckman's personal file." She read off the number. The area code was for eastern Massachusetts. The exchange was familiarly Bostonian. I wrote down the ten figures, thanked the woman for her cooperation and promised to be back to Mr. Druckman if I heard anything further.

"I'm sure he'll be pleased," the woman said. "So will Mr. Elfinstone."

"We're hopeful, ourselves," I said, feeling triumphant. "We'll keep our fingers crossed."

My fingers were already doing the walking. I had grabbed the Boston phone book and was flipping it open to the Es. I thanked the woman and hung up. And found Elfinstone, Charles. On Joy Street. With the same number that Master Artists Corporation had provided.

But who the hell was he? The triumph turned dull and then sour. I'd never heard of Charles Elfinstone. And if he wasn't a patient or a friend or even an acquaintance, what was he doing in this room?

Or, more precisely, what else could he have been doing? The book was clear enough. Brad Steele, his hero, had been burglarizing, investigating, rummaging through the files. Was the burglarizing as true as the horse and the watch and the etching?

It still didn't make a whole lot of sense. If he had broken in, why had he written about it? And published it? A fruitcake! I mean, psychiatry makes sense out of various kinds of mental illness and hallucination and all manner of odd behavior. But there is some behavior that makes no sense at all. And that's fruitcake behavior! The diagnosis is acute cuckoo!

With what I am afraid was a certain degree of savagery, frustrated as I was by these unyielding considerations, I attacked my cottage cheese. A soothing exercise, for cottage cheese is nonviolent and peaceful. It does not fight back. You can't even chew it very hard.

A few minutes before one, Stanley arrived. There ought to be some graceful way to introduce Stanley, who is himself admirably graceful and tactful. Or at least funny, for he is, in his deadpan way, very funny. He is my secretary, general-helper graduate student, and friend. He was sent over by a student work-program bureau once and we talked for a while, and I was just about to offer him the job when he expressed, with some considerable hesitation, a willingness to consider working for me.

It was a weird tactic and I told him so. "I mean, you are here for a job, aren't you? You're applying for a job. It's assumed you're willing to take the job."

"I don't assume anything," he said, with a very serious shake of his head. "I go to a lot of these interviews for the fun of it, to tell these people that, no, I don't want to work for them. I don't work for Mr. Charlie."

"Mr. Charlie?"

"You're putting me on, Dr. Chayse. You surely are. Mr. Charlie? Whitey?"

"But I'm white."

"But you're a woman. You are oppressed."

"I see," I said.

"You are, whether you see it or not. And I'm willing to take that into account. I'll take the job."

"All right," I said, and solemnly shook his hand.

He was touchy and proud, as all of us are if we are young and bright. But he was also efficient, tough, thoughtful, and generous. He could also type like lightning.

He breezed in wearing a pair of mirror sunglasses and a wasp-waisted Edwardian blazer, said a courtly "Good afternoon, Dr. Chayse," picked up the tray and was on his way out to the kitchen with it when I stopped him.

"Stanley, why would anybody break in here?"

"Did someone break in here?"

"I think so."

"Today? Last night?" He put the tray down.

"A year and a half ago. Maybe two years."

He picked up the tray again.

"I'm serious," I said.

"You've been meaning to mention it to me and it slipped your mind? You're going to think about it for another couple of years and call the police? What are you talking about?"

"Here, read this."

I handed him the book. He put the tray back down and read the page to which the book was open. The beginning of the third chapter. He read it quickly, and looked around. Then he read it again. Then he looked at the cover of the book.

"Who is Greg Pitman?" he asked.

"His real name is Charles Elfinstone. He lives in Boston. On Joy Street."

"A patient? A friend?"

"I've never heard of him."

"And you think he broke in here?"

"Where else would he get those particular details?"

"I don't know. In the book it's a break-in?"

"For blackmail. For information about the files."

He didn't say anything. He didn't have to. His low whistle was sufficiently expressive.

"I wish I could think of some other explanation. I've tried," I said.

"It's too bad. It really is. I wanted to like the guy, this Pitman cat. I mean, he's got a name that's even worse than mine."

"There's nothing wrong with your name," I told him.

"Nothing wrong with it? It's supposed to be an African name, for God's sake. My grandmother figured it out. It was all she knew about Africa. What the hell kind of name for a black boy in America is Stanley Livingstone, anyway?"

"I never thought . . ." I began to say. But there was no way to go on. We were both laughing.

Three

"What do I do?" I asked. "Call the police?"

"And what do they do?" he asked. "Arrest the book?"

"They might go and talk with Elfinstone."

"And what do you think he's going to tell them? Come on! There's just no way. The cops aren't going to believe there was a crime in the first place, and even if they do, Elfinstone isn't going to admit anything. Think about it. A policeman with a book? It's already pretty funny."

"I suppose," I said.

"You suppose? Poor Dr. Chayse! You believe in the police, don't you. You think they're just like those friendly guys on TV? Tough on the outside but with hearts of gold, crusading against evil and all that jazz? They got better things to do than worry about a page in a book. The only kind of book they know is the one the bagman hits on Fridays. They got money to pick up. They're not going to worry about some guy who looked at your blue horse a year ago."

"All right, I agree with you. It was silly. But what else is there to do? Forget it?"

"You could. I guess the question really is whether anybody in those files has been bothered. Who would have been vulnerable a year ago? Who had secrets in there that were really dangerous? If nobody was hurt, then, yes, you forget about it."

"Or I could go and talk to Elfinstone."

"Nancy Drew? You? You think he's going to tell you any more than he would tell the fuzz?"

"No, but perhaps I can listen better than they can. I'm supposed to be able to do that, after all."

"You also could get hurt better than they do."

"I don't think so. If he attacked me, I mean physically attacked me, that would be admitting a crime. Committing one, but admitting the other one. And then I'd have something to go to the police to complain about. They'd have to pay attention then. And he wouldn't want that."

"If you could still go to the police . . ."

"Well, I've never had to use it, but I have always wondered if those judo lessons are any good. Maybe I could find out."

"Judo lessons? You never told me about any judo lessons."

"Oh, yes. At the Women's Center. Every Wednesday night. I wanted to take a dancing class, but modern dance was on Tuesday nights, and Tuesdays I have the Symphony. So I took judo instead. For the exercise, mostly. But it's supposed to be useful. And political. We're supposed to be able to defend ourselves."

"So you don't believe in the police, after all?" Stanley asked.

"I don't know. It's never come up for me before. I suppose the other possibility is a private detective."

"I don't think so," he said. "Anybody who took the case the way it is now would just be out to fleece you. Anyone any good would throw you out of the office. A page in a book? That's all you've got!"

I thought for a minute. "No, it isn't that so much," I said. "It's even worse. If there was a crime, the victim had to be a patient. The way to look for the crime is in those files. Talk to Elfinstone, maybe, but also look in the files. And I'm not sure I want anyone else doing that—policeman, private detective, anyone. I'm not even sure I have the right to open those files."

"You want me to talk to Elfinstone?" Stanley offered. "Or to come with you?"

"No, I'd better do it myself."

"What if he does have a gun? He could. The world is full of crazy people."

"I know that, Stanley."

"I guess you do."

It was a joke, but neither one of us could summon up a smile for it. He took the tray and a pile of cassettes to transcribe. I turned my attention to my patients. It was five minutes to one. There were four of them to see. The first would be arriving any time.

"What you could do," I said, as he was about to leave, "is go through the appointment books for the year before last. And maybe the year before that. A list of names. It's a start."

"Will do."

I heard the door opening. My first patient had arrived. I reached into the desk, pulled out a bottle of cologne, splashed it on my neck and forehead, and turned my cooled and refreshed attention to somebody else's problems.

At five, done for the day, my last notes dictated into the cassette recorder, I went into the study to find the list Stanley had prepared. Attached to it with a paper clip there was a three-by-five card on which, in various colors with a collection of soft-tipped pens, Stanley had left a message: BE CAREFUL!!! A kindly thought.

Phone first? Or simply appear at his door. It would be more prudent to telephone, but then, what could I possibly say? I did not want to put him on his guard. I thought about it, and deciding that it was ridiculous to be so scrupulous—had he been?—I dialed the number, waited for the connection, waited two rings, and then heard a male voice say, "Hello?"

"Is Mr. Underwood there, please?"

"What number do you want?" he asked.

I recited his number, but reversed the last two digits.

"I'm afraid you've misdialed," he said, and hung up.

So, he was there. And unless I planned to extend this one foray to an entire campaign of wrong numbers, crank calls, heavy breathing and the like, I was committed to go. Now. And felt? Apprehensive, of course, but also slightly amused. It was such a curious thing to be doing. Unfamiliar and at the same time, with all those television programs and movies, terribly banal. I looked out the window, saw that the day which had begun well was now gray and threatening. There was no other way around it. I went to the closet inside the front door, put on a trench coat, made a Roz Russell *moue* in the mirror and walked out. I drove into Boston and parked under the common. I climbed up to the greensward, and then trudged up Beacon Hill to Joy Street.

Elfinstone's house was one of those impressive Federal structures, once a private residence, now cut up into apartments. I had been in some of these apartments. They tended to be small, expensive, inconvenient—the streets on Beacon Hill are treacherous in the winter, even with the handrails—but the area is still impressive, with its silly gaslights and all that history crammed into a few blocks. I have, as you see, mixed feelings about it.

My feelings aside, there were practical considerations. A good house in an expensive neighborhood. If Elfinstone had in fact broken into my office, it was not likely to have been for money. The rents here were as steep as the streets themselves. On the other hand, that might mean it was easier to fall behind . . .

There were five apartments in the building. Elfinstone was on the third floor. I pushed the button, waited, heard an answering buzz, and opened the inner door. There was a fine carved staircase and good lighting. Paintings on the landings. I climbed the second flight of stairs. He was peering out through a partly opened door.

"Yes?"

"Mr. Elfinstone?"

"Yes."

"My name is Chayse," I said. "Sarah Chayse."

"Yes?"

"I'd like to talk to you for a moment about *Do Not Go Gentle*. You are Greg Pitman, aren't you?"

"Am I?"

"Mr. Druckman's office gave me your name."

"Well, far be it from me to contradict Mr. Druckman. Whoever he is."

"Of Master Artists Corporation. Your agents?"

"I see," he said. But he didn't say anything else or do anything further. He was undecided. He was in his forties somewhere. From the head and the upper half of his body that protruded from the doorway, he seemed to be in good physical shape. His hair was receding slightly. But he was slender, rather pale—although that could have been the light—and, more to the point, harmless-looking. Certainly no great bruiser of an athlete.

"You want to talk about a book?" he asked.

"Just for a few minutes. If you can spare that."

"All right, why not? Come on in."

He held the door open and stood aside. I entered his apartment. The living room registered as somehow impromptu, accidental. The pieces of furniture had nothing to do with one another. Good pieces, some of them, but they stood next to one another like strangers, like orphans in a showroom waiting to be bought. The Chinese Chippendale desk might have been authentic. But the Eames chair was a copy. And there were travel posters taped to the white walls. On the other wall, there was a good grandfather clock in cherry, and next to it one of those plastic Parsons tables from Woolworth's. Irrational. Unless of course the good pieces were what Elfinstone had salvaged from a broken marriage, filling in however he could with whatever came to hand. He got the clock and the desk, while she took the paintings? Something like that?

I sat down in the Eames copy. He sat down behind his good desk, hiding behind it, taking security from it. I studied him for a moment. No, I had never seen the man before. Never.

"I'm a doctor," I said. "A psychiatrist. I have an office in my house in Cambridge. You've been in the office."

"In your office?"

"Apparently. That's why I came to see you. I can't place you. And I'm curious about your familiarity with my office."

"I'm afraid I don't understand you. I don't think I've been in your office, actually . . ."

"You described it. In your book."

"All offices are much the same, aren't they?"

"Do you have the book?"

"Somewhere."

"If you'll take a look at what you wrote, you'll see that this is a particular office, carefully described. There is a small lapis-lazuli horse. There is an old pocket watch. There's an etching."

"And you have all these things?"

"Yes. I have them, and they are arranged in exactly the way you describe."

"What an extraordinary coincidence!"

"Is it?"

"Of course it is. I've never been in your office."

"How could you have described the etching then?"

"I must have seen it in a gallery. It's an etching, after all. There are other copies. I must have seen one in one of those galleries on Newberry Street."

"And the horse?"

"The world is full of horses. And watches."

"With stands worked in vine leaves?"

"A conventional design. Like acanthus moldings."

"It's difficult to believe . . ."

"Then what do you believe? That I'm lying? Why should I?"

A nervous smile flashed on and off again, like a "Don't Walk" sign.

"In the book, the office is broken into . . ."

"I see," Elfinstone said. "Well, suppose I had broken into your office, although I can't imagine why I'd do such a thing. But suppose I had. Would I then describe the office that way? Wouldn't I be careful to conceal these details? What sense would there be in my writing it down and having it published?"

"I don't know. A plea for help, perhaps? 'Stop me before I burgle again.' That kind of thing."

"I'm afraid not. No, it doesn't figure. Look at it the other way. How do I know that your office has these things? How do I know that these things were there two years ago, when I was writing the book? I have to trust you, don't I? But you don't trust me. There doesn't seem to be much of a basis for discussion, does there?"

I waited a beat. He would get up, would usher me out, would terminate the interview. But he made no move. A challenge, then? An invitation for me to continue? Had there been a plea for help?

"Why did you use a pseudonym?" I asked gently.

"One tries to hide one's crimes," he said, flashing the smile again. "It's not a very good book," he explained. "It wasn't even a book at all. It was a treatment for a film. The paperback was a way of recouping something for the time I had put in. But it wasn't anything like what I'd want to sign. I do write real books sometimes," and he gestured with a wave to a shelf in the bookcase behind him.

"I see," I said. "It was just a business thing, then?"

"A purely literary crime. Something to keep the wolf from the door during a bit of a dry spell I've been having."

"Long?"

"What? The dry spell? Not terribly. It happens to all of us now and then. Or most of us. Most writers. I'm out of it, I think. Working again. Feeling good. That was a couple of years ago, after all."

"And how does one break through?" I asked.

"Oh, any way that works. I just think about other things. Go for a trip. Change the scene. No mystery to it, I'm afraid. Wait it out."

"Simple as that?"

"If you're lucky. I was."

But had he been? His thumb and finger were pill-rolling in apprehension, just thinking about it. And what kind of change of scene was

23

it to do potboilers under another name? Point this out, or not? I didn't want to push him too hard.

"Have you used other pen names?" I asked.

"No. Never had the occasion."

"So if I wanted to read something of yours, I'd look under your real name?"

"That would be the way to do it, yes."

"I shall, indeed. May I use your bathroom?"

"Surely," he said.

He got up and led the way down a small corridor. Through an open door I could see his bedroom, a double-bed mattress on the floor, and a piece of a brick-and-plank bookcase with a hi-fi amplifier on it. More salvage? Or had there been more furniture, more art, things he'd had to sell or pawn off?

I went into the bathroom and closed and locked the door behind me. A foolish maneuver, perhaps, but it had struck me in the living room that there might be some bits of information I could glean in here. Anyway, it had seemed worth trying. I turned on the cold water, and as it ran I looked in the medicine cabinet. Curiously, there was almost nothing in it. Shaving cream, a razor, a hairbrush, a comb (none too clean), shampoo, toothpaste, aspirin, antiperspirant, Preparation-H, mouthwash . . . But no prescription drugs? No sleeping pills? No medicines of any kind? Not even the end of an old bottle of codeine pills. I looked at the razor, which he stored in its original plastic case. On the bottom was a price sticker he had never bothered to remove from the Bowdoin Pharmacy.

A Christian Scientist, perhaps? No, there were the aspirins and the Preparation-H for his hemorrhoids.

I closed the medicine-cabinet door, flushed the toilet, turned off the faucet and left the bathroom.

"Thank you," I said. "You've been very kind."

"Not at all. I'm flattered, really. It's a small thing, but for a writer to dream up a room and then find out that it exists . . . Well, it's satisfying. It shows I'm paying attention."

"I'm looking forward to reading one of the books you liked well enough to sign."

"I hope you find something to like," he said.

I did not offer my hand, nor did he, his. I left the apartment and walked down the stairs, down the hill, and toward the common. It

24

was drizzling but not cold. Anyway, I had my trench coat. I felt like walking, felt the need to clear my head.

No, he had not been telling the truth. No matter how much he protested, there could not be such a coincidence. The horse and the watch and the etching. And the powder-blue files. But why should he be looking into my files? For himself? For someone else? It was not inconceivable that he was in need of money, that he had been in worse need two years ago . . .

If he had broken in, then his self-possession was extraordinary for an amateur. He had been a little too careful at the beginning, but then, as soon as he had decided how to proceed, he had carried himself quite well. A little nervous, and yet . . . I wondered if he was on something. But there had been nothing in the medicine cabinet. Odd.

There was no point in worrying it. I knew better than that. The thing to do was to think of other things, think about nothing at all, walk fast enough so that the strenuousness of the exercise turned my mind to idle. I stepped up my pace and walked along the path through the gardens. I passed the Ritz and thought of going in for tea. But then the idea of tea connected up to the idea of Chinese food. That was what I wanted. Szechwan spicy bean curd and pots of tea. I went over to the parking garage, drove across the river to Joyce Chen's, had myself a gorge, and felt much better.

It was only toward the end of the meal that I tried to assess my position. I would go back home and look at Stanley's list, watching out for possible connections, no matter how remote, between one of my patients and Elfinstone. If there was a connection, then it would be simple enough to follow it up. And if not?

Could I believe him? A nervous writer with no tranquilizers, no sedatives, nothing at all in his medicine chest but aspirin? A blocked writer who got through his block by writing potboilers?

"Why did you use a pseudonym?" I remembered asking.

And he had answered, "One tries to hide one's crimes."

I looked out the window at the lights of Boston reflected in the river. My waiter brought me a fortune cookie. I opened it up. The message said I was thorough and persistent and that was the secret of my success.

Four

In my study, with a bottle of rainwater Madeira and a bowl of walnuts, and with a stack of Haydn symphonies on the record player, I considered the list before me. Or considered considering it. It does not do to attack such projects too directly. In matters of judgment, mood is important, and the tastes of the wine and the walnuts were comforting, familiar delights. The crispness of Haydn, the cheerfully sensuous sanity of that good man's music, helped to ward off paranoid fears. Talismans against the darkness, perhaps, but helpful. As long as I could remain light and cheerful about this odd business, I would be all right, judge properly, be able to trust myself. If I thought of it as an intellectual problem, a kind of game . . . The danger was always there, and I could see it plainly enough, that I become too intimately involved in the problems of my patients, take them onto my own shoulders and spirit, and by so doing, be less able to help them. There was an opposite danger as well, that of becoming altogether professional, calloused, indifferent. "Teach us to care and not to care./ Teach us to sit still," Eliot wrote, and it ought to be part of the Hippocratic Oath for psychiatrists. For all doctors.

On a sheet of paper, in Stanley's improbably delicate hand, there was a list of names. Of ailments and of griefs. Varieties of loneliness and despair, the torments of living, and the answers the mind could make in depression or delusion.

I took a sip of the Madeira and cracked a walnut shell. The eating of walnuts can be a great pleasure, for there is an art in the extraction of the whorled lobes of meat from the hard shells. Too eager, too strong, and one can make a mess of a walnut, but a correctly cracked,

26

deftly extracted walnut meat is an achievement. Concentrate on the small graces and the larger problems will sometimes yield. Returning my attention to that list, it seemed somehow much simpler. Who was vulnerable to blackmail? Very few, actually. The depressives who were afraid of middle age, afraid of dying, afraid that their lives were closing down, the people who could not believe that this is all there is . . . They were not blackmail subjects. Nor were the frigid, nor the impotent, nor the terrified. I had to look for the people who acted out, whose defenses and reactions involved some external gesture. It would only be in very special circumstances that the mere fact of treatment by a psychiatrist would be a matter for blackmail. As in the terrible business with Senator Eagleton. Which was reason to put a check next to Senator Farnsworth's name. He was only a state senator, but Massachusetts politics could be vicious. And Farnsworth could have hopes of higher offices. A possibility.

Philip Drexel? He was a homosexual, rather well adjusted and with a stable enough life, threatened suddenly by the decision of the board of trustees of the girls' school of which he was headmaster to go coed. A touchy business, and for Drexel, a real threat. As a headmaster of a girls' school, he was perfectly safe, effective, competent. With boys, he could still be effective, but he was worried, had begun to doubt himself, to feel worthless and useless. He could be vulnerable.

Patricia Kearns? Not likely for her to be the subject of blackmail, or not the way I had been thinking about it. But Patricia was an occasion for blackmail. Any of the men from whom she took reassurance and to whom, in turn, she bestowed her sexual favors might be victims. Patricia had been a patient until very recently, when she had improved considerably and gone off to school. But the break-in had been two years ago, and there were a number of men, prominent in Boston, who had behaved badly. Statutory rape, technically. And of a girl under psychiatric care. It could be . . .

Others I dismissed. I ran thick lines through the names of those whose ailments were in no way yielding to the greed—for money? power? favors?—of a blackmailer. And then I hesitated again. I had been about to run a line through Dwayne French's name, on the ground that the man was dead and safe from harm. But two years ago? He had come to me with a pathological fear of flying, of which I had managed to cure him. At any rate, he had sufficiently benefited from therapy to go up in planes and to lose his life in a crash. But he had used cocaine, an upper-middle-class drug but still dangerous for a securities dealer. It was certainly worth a check mark.

It was mostly the fact that French was dead that led me to Adam Swett. He, too, was dead. Of a heart attack. More than two years ago? Rather less. A year and a half? Something like that. I'd read the obituary in the Boston *Globe*. He had not been a patient for very long, had come in with lethargy as a reaction to stress. The stress was certainly reasonable enough, for Swett had been Harvard's first black dean, and had presided over—and perhaps been destroyed by —the activist year of demonstrations and protests, the object of which had been to gain a larger share in the university for blacks. And they'd killed off their dean. Swett had discontinued therapy after a short and indeterminate trial. But I remembered that—during the Korean War—he had been in his youth a numbers runner and occasional procurer in Detroit. I could not imagine who else would have known such details about Swett's early life. And there had been no mention of these things in my files. But I could not rule out the possibility that someone had come looking. I was not convinced, did not think it likely that a Harvard dean could be blackmailed. Certainly not for money. And Swett had died quite normally of a heart attack. Still, what I thought was likely did not necessarily correspond to the tastes and standards of a man like Elfinstone. A check mark, then.

I refilled the glass. I listened to the energy of Max Goberman's performance of the Haydn. Not normal, certainly, but healthy. Health is rare, after all. Which of us is altogether sound? The elegant variation of the second violins playing about the melodic line of the first violins, while the sober cello section marked the outlines of the pattern . . . No life has so decorous, so decorative a shape. I looked at the list once more. No, not him. Or her. Or him. Slash, slash, the pen went through the names. And then I paused once more. Cora Hubbard? She had rebelled against the diminutions of age, her deteriorating digestion, her menopause, by developing a fondness for gambling. Not at all a question for psychoanalysis, really, but her sister had been concerned and had pushed Cora into a series of interviews with me. The sister believed that all gambling was crazy, and that all gamblers therefore needed psychiatric help. Cora was not crazy. And she was a sharp, tough woman who pointed out in our first conversation that she generally lost less at the blackjack table in an hour than she spent to talk with me. Still, for a chief teller, there were obvious reasons for wanting to keep the gambling habit a secret. A check mark with a little question mark beside it.

I spent five symphonies—Haydn symphonies are short—looking at the names on the list, examining the rest, reexamining those I had crossed out. But I was satisfied that the most likely possibilities were those I had selected. In none of those names could I see any connection with Elfinstone. But then I knew very little about Elfinstone's life. I would have to read some of his books, find out more about him.

I remembered the Bowdoin Pharmacy. I turned the record player off and telephoned the pharmacy. I identified myself, and asked the pharmacist to check back in his records to let me know who was Charles Elfinstone's doctor.

"It may take a little while," the pharmacist told me. "If you could leave your number, I'd be happy to call you back as soon as I've had a chance to look through the books."

"Certainly," I said. I spelled my name and left my telephone number. I understood that he wanted to be sure that there was a Dr. Sarah Chayse, that I was listed, had a phone . . . I approved, entirely.

"As soon as I can," he promised.

"You're very kind," I said.

Felicity came wandering into the room, a great white puff of a cat with evil green eyes . . . Well, not really evil, but she did enjoy killing. All that wonderful grace, that lithe ability to leap up three and four times her height to a kitchen cabinet or from there to the top of the refrigerator, and with the effortlessness of a thought, and it was all equipment for murder. A gorgeous savage, and yet affectionate. She would, from time to time, take notice of me, sit with me, even rub against my legs. She appeared now, stretched herself in a Halloween hump, and sat, staring.

Endorsing this absurd project? I recognized that the likelihood of finding out anything interesting, either from the druggist or from the doctor—if Elfinstone had a doctor—was remote indeed. And yet there were lessons to be learned from Felicity. To notice a slight movement, to stalk so slowly and so silently as to float across a floor, to sit motionless for the longest time with a patience that could be a weapon. I had learned to sit for months at the mental mouseholes waiting for patients' psyches to show themselves. With the external world there has to be the same kind of patience. And the same willingness to follow up all sorts of suggestions, to ask all sorts of questions, most of which would turn out to be irrelevant and pointless.

I realized that I had emotionally written off the druggist. He would not call. Or if he did, he would have no information. Or the information would be useless. Silly to sit and wait for it. Let Felicity sit and wait. I got up, put the papers into a folder, put the folder into a drawer, and gathered up the wine bottle, wineglass and the walnut bowl, and started toward the kitchen.

Of course, the phone rang. I put down the bottle, the glass, and the bowl, picked up the phone, and with the other hand, reached into the polished copper mug that held fountain pens, soft-tip markers, pencils, ball-points, and grabbed one. "Yes?"

"Dr. Chayse? This is the Bowdoin Pharmacy."

"Oh, yes." The pen I had grabbed was out of ink. I was looking for another. I found a Bic Banana, in a garish purple, which had come free in a box of Ajax.

"We've looked through our records. It took a while. There aren't very many prescriptions at all for Mr. Elfinstone. But we did find one, for a penicillin suspension. About a year ago."

"Fine," I said. "I appreciate it. And who was the prescribing doctor?"

"Dr. Harney. James F."

"I see. Thank you very much indeed. You've been most helpful."

"Anything we can do, any time . . ."

"I appreciate it." I hung up.

So he had a sore throat or something, and he went to a doctor and got some penicillin. But then, what had I expected? A series of massive doses of morphine? Huge quantities of sleeping pills?

I was at a dead end. Nothing to do but go the other way, to check out the names on my list. Perhaps one of them had been pushed, had been squeezed somehow . . . Perhaps there would be a line that led, either directly or indirectly, back to Elfinstone. If not? I could drop it.

I picked up the bottle, the glass, and the bowl, and I started back toward the kitchen. Again, the phone rang, and again I lay my burdens down and picked up the telephone.

"Yes?"

"Sarah? Martin. How are you?"

"Okay. Preoccupied."

"A bad time? Shall I call back?"

"No, no. Not occupied. Preoccupied."

"Elegant, but what does it mean? You have time to talk, but not to listen?"

"Elegant, yourself! Listen, can I ask you a favor?"

"Sure."

"Two favors?"

"What is it, an auction? You can ask me nine favors. Twenty-three favors! A hundred and four favors . . ."

"Just two. Just one, really, but two parts. And the catch part is that I don't want you to ask any questions."

"Okay."

"Can you find out what the word is on Dr. James F. Harney?"

"I can try, sure. But . . ."

"But no questions."

"Can't I even ask what I'm supposed to find out about him?"

"Anything at all. What his reputation is. What he smells like."

"Sniff around."

"Exactly."

"He's here in Boston, I assume. That's not a question, I remind you, merely a statement of an assumption, open to correction if necessary."

"Yes, he's here in Boston."

"Okay. You want to know what the word is on you?"

"What word?"

"That you're spooky. Nuts."

"I always speak well of you, dear."

"I take what I can get," he said, and then, after a beat, "but . . . Are you all right? I mean, you sound funny."

"No questions."

"I assume the conference went well?"

"It was fine."

"It's nice that you're back. That's actually why I called. To say that."

"Thank you. It's good to be back. It's good of you to call."

"Dinner Friday might be nice. That's not a question!"

"It might be. I'll let you know."

"Good. I'll call you. With the word on the sniff."

"Thanks."

Dear Martin. Natty, handsome, energetic, he was still a kind of puppy dog. Or, no, that's too diminishing. Boyish, in ways. And we fenced and sparred, liking each other, trying to balance off our liking of each other with our liking of our selves, our own lives, the delicate arrangements we had made with the world for our own survival. After Roger, I was reluctant to make the same kind of leap. I didn't have that dumb faith any more, or maybe I just didn't have the energy. And Martin wavered, himself. Sometimes he could breathe hard, wanting more of a bond. And then he could back away. Or seem to, as the demands of his work gobbled up his time and attention.

In a way, John was a kind of anchor for me. Even for both of us. As if I needed one. I had a pageant of mangled, savaged lives parading through my offices every day. Men and women have a difficult time together, and the more they expect, the less likely they are to find what they are looking for. The prudent thing is to settle for less. And I suppose the best that could be said for the arrangement I had contrived with Martin and with John was that I could live with it for a while. How many of us can claim even that?

I picked up the first of the files. Drexel's. I started to read it, realized that I had read the same paragraph four times, and did the only sensible thing, putting it down and letting it go. I was tired. I fed Felicity and went upstairs to bed.

Five

The difficulty with Phil Drexel was that I couldn't come right out and ask him if anyone had tried to blackmail him without running the risk that the question could wound him seriously. He was a nervous man, and there was enough real substance to his complaint that the world was conspiring unfairly against him to make it a matter of some delicacy for me to add even a little to the burden of fears and worries he carried around with his Harvard bookbag. His was a most painful, most unfair situation. Twenty years younger or twenty years older, and there would have been a clear role for him to play, a more or less acceptable pattern of behavior. But the poor dear was caught halfway out of the closet by a society which was enlightened enough to recognize him for what he was but not yet willing to approve or condone. Under the old willful blindness, or under the expected enlightenment, he could have some reasonable idea of what was expected of him, and could find some appropriate response . . .

Still, he was a clever enough fellow. He had come to me with feelings of persecution and paranoia, but he had recognized them for what they were. It can take months to get a patient that far, and he had made the difficult connections on his own. He was entitled to be pleased with himself, and he was. I remember his claim that it takes a certain degree of imagination to be a paranoid, a kind of flair. Beyond the jokes, however, there was the real feeling, and the feeling was not pleasant. Guilt displaced, torment made visible, flashing in other eyes and across other faces like warning signals in a menacing night.

We had worked through it, and we had made enough progress for him to go back to the struggle on his own. I was available if he needed me, but he had an idea that therapy was like a crutch and that one ought not to be too dependent on it. Not wholly implausible.

Touchy, then, to call him. And no doubt it would be alarming for him to know what my concern was. Still, there were other ways to go about the task. I had a light morning at the clinic, and late-afternoon appointments. There was a hole in the middle of the day and I could use it, drive out through Belmont and Concord and just stop by on the way through . . . He might not believe it, might assume that I was coming by to check up on him and see how he was. But there was nothing wrong with that. It was perfectly appropriate and probably something psychiatrists ought to do anyway. I could show interest, be supportive. Better to spend my time doing that than in administrative meetings at the clinic. Hell, better to spend time walking by the river and watching the sculls.

I drove out there, announced myself to the receptionist in the fake-Tudor administration building that had once been the main residence of some tycoon's estate, and sat down on a carved oak bench that had certainly not been there when the tycoon had owned the place. The receptionist announced me, and almost immediately Phil Drexel's door opened.

"How good to see you! Come in, come in."

He closed the door behind me.

"I was passing by," I said. "I'd never seen the school. I thought I'd come in to say hello."

"Very likely," he said, with a conspiratorial smile. "But that's all right. I don't mind. It really is good to see you. And I appreciate your tact."

"My tact?"

"You gave your name but not your title. Sarah Chayse. Not Dr. Chayse. Very nice, very thoughtful. But not necessary. I have decided to retire."

"Oh?"

"That was the problem all along, I think. Not the other thing. I want to change my life, to live it a little bit. I'm leaving at the end of the year, and I shall go to Cyprus to work on an archeological dig and to write a bit . . . I'm quite happy about it."

"A voluntary retirement?" I asked.

"Absolutely. And it's because it's a free choice that I can do it, don't you see? I mean, I could have stayed on here. Even with the

34

boys in the school. I may be gay but I'm not a maniac. It's exactly what straights have to deal with when they teach girls."

"But no outside pressure."

"No."

"I'm glad. About your decision, I mean. It should be fun."

"I can't tell you how alive I feel. New prospects, new horizons . . . It's quite giddy. Can you stay for lunch?"

"I wish I could. But I have to get back. I have meetings all afternoon."

"Perhaps later on, then. Before I go off to Cyprus. We might have dinner. I'd be very pleased."

"Yes, so would I," I told him truthfully. We shook hands and he saw me out to the foyer.

I got into the car, started back toward Cambridge, and turned the entire process of driving to automatic pilot. I was pleased about Phil Drexel's decision, and yet disappointed, too. How dumb I'd been. What kind of possible scenario could I have devised in order to connect his situation to a blackmailer or to a burglar? It made no sense. Did any of the others? Was the entire episode a lapse of judgment, a figment of my imagination? Was I as sane as I ought to be?

At any rate, he was out of it. He'd made his decision and it was not a bad one. He'd extorted honorable terms from the world, and then had settled for a decent retirement. I could imagine him blooming quite nicely in some Mediterranean setting, with those attractive sailors and strong crude wines to divert him from his writing and his digging. He might be much happier there, more at home than in his native New England.

The thing that bothered me was the wispiness of this pursuit of some connection between a patient of mine and Charles Elfinstone. If blackmail was not the connection, then anything could be, and every name in my files would be a potential subject. Still, it seemed only logical to rule out the first half-dozen names that had presented themselves to my attention and intuition. I was not losing any ground, surely.

I stopped at a Burger King for a Whopper, getting the usual surprised question when I asked them to hold the meat. The salad and the dressing make a respectable sandwich, and from what I'm told, I'm not missing that much meat anyway. Scarcely enough to notice, at any rate.

Back in my study, I called Cora Hubbard, but she was no longer at the bank. I called her home. The number had been disconnected. I called her sister's number. There was no answer.

There were, of course, reasonable explanations. But I found that I was rather drawn toward unreasonable ones, toward danger and menace. What could have happened to Cora Hubbard? No longer at the bank, no longer living in the apartment across the hall from her sister? Had she lost huge sums at the gambling tables? Had there been one of those enforcer types from organized crime and the gambling syndicate threatening her? Had she fled in terror of her life, to start another existence under another name in some other city, or even some other country? Had the enforcer come to my files in an attempt to track her down?

It did not seem plausible, but then the damned thing was that I couldn't judge what was plausible and what wasn't. One is not prepared to hunch the probabilities of crime unless one has some experience of crime, or of its detection. I could only speculate blindly, and try to be patient. I called the sister back, and again got no answer. I turned my attention to other things, read some notes I needed to look at for my afternoon's patients, and saw three of them in three hours, trying the number each time in the ten-minute break the schedule allowed me.

It was nearly seven by the time I got through to her. I asked what had happened to Cora, where she was living now, how she was. I was rewarded with the information that Cora had married a widower, had moved to Newton, and was fine. I was provided with Cora's married name—Rumford—and invited to call her at a number the sister gave me. So much for syndicate enforcers and desperate flights to elude their clutches.

It was odd that she had married. Not what I might have expected. She had not appeared to be at all sexual. And yet, this is never true. Everyone is sexual. Some of us find it necessary to hide sexuality—even, sometimes, from ourselves. And assume that she had done so, and assume that her motive was fear. Then, after menopause, with nothing to worry about, no risk of pregnancy, she might begin to unfold a little, come out like the belated butterfly from her fretful cocoon. Not at all unlikely. And remembering things about Cora, recalling things she'd said during her visits, it seemed more and more likely. I was pleased for her. I had another name to cross off my list, but I was glad it was hers.

Is there a relation between the fear of getting knocked up and the pleasures of gambling? Something to wonder about, someday.

Meanwhile, there was my diminishing list of possible victims. Senator Farnsworth? Not unlikely. A local manifestation of Watergate could explain a burglary for his records. Patty Kearns? A less promising, less probable target, unless she was being used to get to someone else, one of her lovers. And then there were my two dead men, Dwayne French and Adam Swett. I ran them through my mind, quickly, and got nothing, no reaction at all. The elimination of Cora Hubbard Rumford and of Phil Drexel did not seem to make any of them more likely or less likely. Still, I had to play out the string. I called Senator Farnsworth at home, told him I wanted to see him, and set up an appointment for lunch the next day. I'd decided to level with him. No particular reason not to, and a lot of reasons for telling the truth, not the least of which was the chance to get some other reaction, some other response. If he told me that I was being alarmist and unreasonable . . . Would that change anything? I wasn't sure. On the other hand, he might have some suggestions for doing better what I was trying to do. On the phone, I told him that there was a kind of an intellectual problem I was having, and I needed his help.

"I'm most flattered," he said. "And of course, I'd be happy to help in any way I can. Is twelve-thirty all right for you?"

I told him that was fine, and I'd meet him in his office downtown.

He sounded perfectly cheerful, entirely calm. Not the way the victim of some dark plot of extortion or blackmail would sound in a movie. Of course, it was possible that the victim didn't know what had happened, or that nothing had happened. It was conceivable that the scheme—whatever it was—had aborted, that nothing had actually happened at all. Or that there had been a break-in and nothing else. And only then had Elfinstone decided to recoup somehow and turn the original scheme into the plot of a book. Or a piece of the plot. The nonsense about spies could have nothing to do with any of the people who had come into my office or left their traces in my files.

It was dark. I turned on lights and went to the kitchen to make myself an omelette, chill some wine, and sit down to a civilized, solitary supper.

I was washing up afterwards when Martin called.

"You busy?" he asked. "I've got some stuff for you. About Harney."

"No, not busy at all," I told him.

"You want to hear it on the phone, or shall I come over? I can be there in ten minutes."

"Why not?" I said. "Actually, I could use some advice. Some help, even."

"I'll be right there."

He appeared fifteen minutes later, carrying a bottle of champagne in a cooler full of ice.

"What's that for?" I asked.

"For us. For fun. And for the smugness of it. I've discovered this wonderful cheap stuff. It's bulk process, and it's . . . well, the ginger ale of champagnes. But it makes terrific champagne cocktails. Never liked the idea of messing up good champagne with sugar and bitters, but then, I've always liked champagne cocktails. I thought I'd share my discovery with you. Turn you into a wino. And then, desperate to put your life back together, you'll turn to me for help and comfort. Good plan?"

"What about you? Won't you have turned into a wino too?"

"All right, for company, then. I don't care."

"I do."

"Let's drink to that," he said. "You have bitters? Sugar?"

I did. We went into the kitchen and I got them out for him. He muddled the sugar and bitters into champagne glasses, and then opened the bottle with that lovely pop. "Incredible stuff," he said. "Two bucks a bottle, and it's not at all bad. It isn't Taitinger, but you can swill it. Cook sauerkraut in it. Ever had sauerkraut in champagne?"

"No."

"Oh, Sarah, Sarah, there are so many things I want to share with you."

"You do, Martin."

"You know what I mean."

"Are you getting serious again?"

"I'm always serious," he said. "I pretend to joke with you, but you know I'm serious."

"Yes, I know. And I'm serious too."

"I know," he said. And he raised his glass. "To us?"

"Us."

In a way, he was quite sweet. He wanted to marry me. Still does. But I couldn't see the sense to it. Still can't. What on earth for? Neither of us wants children. He has two from his first marriage. I have . . . Well, I have my patients. And other ideas of how to live. Sometimes I think that what Martin really wants is to own me. Or to be owned, which sounds a little nicer but amounts to the same thing. And the way I see it is that we have to make it up as we go along, whether there is a license and an entry in a register somewhere or not. It is also possible that I don't love him enough. I like him. In a way I love him. But . . .

"You want to hear about Dr. Harney?" he asked.

"Please."

"A bad apple. Interesting, maybe. For all I know, he might even be right. But you decide."

"Decide what?"

"Well, you'll see. It's hard to get anyone to come right out with this stuff. Professional ethics and all that shit. But apparently Harney had a decent sort of training, seemed to be a competent man. Should have gone on to be a solid doctor with a decent practice. No great flash, maybe, but how many of us ever are? Anyway, he decided one day that this was not for him, not what he wanted . . . Or maybe he just got tired of sick people. That happens, you know."

"Oh, yes."

"I often think that's why some of the best doctors go into pathology. They can't stand sickness. Slides and cultures. Nice and clean."

"About Harney?"

"He saw the light. Started fooling around with amphetamines, vitamins, hormones. At first it was kind of an overweight clinic. There's lots of money in that. But not very much fun. From there, he went into . . ."

"Into what?"

"I don't know. He's sort of a Doctor Feelgood. Pep pills and hormones and God knows what. He takes people who want to burn brighter and turns them on for a while. It isn't exactly against the law. It isn't even exactly unethical. But it is not considered by most of the good old boys to be quite nice."

"What do you think about it?"

"I don't know. I know what I used to think. I would have hated it once. Now I don't know what I think any more. I have my own problems."

What he meant was his work at furthering emergency medicine as an independent specialty and bringing in the Illinois techniques to Massachusetts. A good thing all around, except that it trod on a lot of people's toes and they didn't like it. And between saving lives and holding on to power, most doctors will hold on to power. Or, in Martin's experience, that was what seemed to be true. He had become a modest kind of crusader after his divorce. The crusade had distracted him at first, kept him occupied. The resistance he had encountered had produced enough legitimate anger to keep the project going, to keep him working at it.

"Here, let me give you a refill," he said.

I gave him my glass.

"You're not thinking of going to him, are you?"

"No."

"Okay. I know I promised not to ask questions. But still . . . You don't mind that one, do you?"

"No, I don't mind. But don't ask me any others. I'll explain it all as soon as I can. A few days. A week maybe."

"Okay," he said, handing me another champagne cocktail. "You know, it's good to see you? I think about you a lot."

"I know," I said. "And it's nice. It helps, sometimes, when I'm tired or depressed, to know that. And when I'm feeling up, it's very nice."

"Oh, shit! I'll never understand you."

"If you did, you might not like me so well."

"Come here," he said.

He kissed me. We left the champagne in the kitchen, its little bubbles streaming up from the bottoms of the glasses. We didn't need them. We had our own.

Six

What a dear, what an absolute dear. Sometime during the night he had folded his tent like the Arabs, and as silently stolen away, but first stopping in the kitchen to tidy up, washing and drying the champagne glasses, putting them away, and removing the bucket and the empty bottle. A habit of discretion? Or merely of neatness? He had, after all, been married, fathered children, been, one might say, domesticated. It was not without its appeal. Of course, it was possible that it was intended to be appealing, but I doubt it. There is a phrase I heard from one of my patients once, that comes either from the German or perhaps the Yiddish. The patient described himself as a man who "pees in a straight line," meaning that he did not work by indirection and stratagem. Martin too.

It is, at any rate, a pleasure to come into a kitchen expecting a little messiness and to find instead a neutral and cheerful tidiness. All traces gone. A new day and a new page. And I found myself wondering whether Martin might not be all right after all. Could he be expected to continue to be so tactful, so understanding, so generous if I married him? Not likely. There is no man so strong as to be able to resist the temptations which are a part of married life. No woman, either. There is a relaxation, not only of mood but of style. We become creatures of each other's habits, and little more.

I made myself an omelette and went off to the clinic. It was a crisp, gorgeous day, and my mood was just fine. I felt so good that I began to doubt what I had been doing. After all, it was perfectly possible that there had been some sort of burglary but that the burglars had found nothing. Nothing at all. One is torn sometimes between possibilities for which there is no hard evidence. One must play hunches, right? But the kinds of hunches are almost certainly going to arise from the kinds of expectations one brings to experience, and to be colored by one's mood at the moment. As good as I was feeling, I could not imagine that anything terrible had happened to anyone. From something in my files? Nonsense! If there had been anything so terrible, so incriminating, so juicy, I'd have remembered it. I'd have thought of it right away. And even if I hadn't, the victim of this break-in surely would have complained to me. These were, after all, my patients. They had come to me for help. In a situation like this, they would have asked for help again.

Possible? Probable? I felt confident enough of it to regret that I had called Senator Farnsworth, that I was going to impose upon him for what might very well be a wholly pointless business. But to call it off? I was not quite so certain as to want to do that. Or perhaps I was apprehensive about the embarrassment of having to explain that the problem was entirely imaginary. Psychiatrists, after all, are supposed to be more or less sane.

I parked in my bay at the clinic, went in to do a brisk morning's work, and then, feeling even sillier than I had in the morning, went to meet the senator.

Farnsworth was a man in his late fifties who had come to me for help during a bad time. Depression, a feeling that his life had been a mistake, a rage that there was nothing else even to hope for, and feelings of worthlessness. It is a common complaint, but no less painful for that, and the difficult part is to make the distinction between the real reasons for sadness (there are often real reasons) and the exaggerated, distorted version of those reasons which the sufferers report. The senator had come through it pretty well. He was not the same man he had been before the depression, but in ways stronger, and gentler. He had developed a wry humor about himself and the world that was not only attractive but even the beginnings of wisdom. There is a kind of adolescent storm—except it isn't adolescent —that hits people in their early fifties. Those who come through it, as Senator Farnsworth had, have a feeling of seaworthiness that lasts for a long time.

He was sitting at an old-fashioned roll-top desk that had once belonged to his father. We'd talked about his father a lot. But he looked quite at home in his office and at that desk, the ancient furniture and the mounted stag head on the wall appearing to be his natural setting. He was one of those angular New Englanders, the bony structure of his cheeks suggesting some sort of tool, ax or adze, and the ranginess of the limbs looking as if they were designed for the use of such tools. He had light-blue eyes, and salt-and-pepper hair, and wore a black suit with a vest, only a little rumpled. He played at being an old codger, but there were little signs that he was only playing. Or maybe it was only that I knew. He seemed, in the mustiness of his inner office, and in that suit and at that desk, to be amused, and therefore, curiously youthful.

"Sarah! How good to see you. How good to see you here, rather than there."

"It's good to see you," I said. "Thank you."

"Not at all, not at all. I ordered sandwiches and coffee. I thought we could eat here. It's quieter than any place we could go. And more private. You don't mind?"

"No, no, that's fine. Thank you."

"My pleasure. Anything I can do . . . But you know that. I ordered egg salad. That's all right, isn't it?"

"That's fine."

Not only had he ordered egg salad for me, but for himself as well. Good manners? Empathy? Probably both. Or maybe he liked egg salad. A lot of non-vegetarians do.

I told him about the mystery, the one in the book and then the one in my own mind. I explained about the improbability of anybody's just making up such a combination of objects as Elfinstone seemed to have invented. I told him about my fears for my files and for the lives of my patients. And I told him a little about my interview with Mr. Elfinstone. I also told him that I had not yet been able to find any indication from anyone I'd talked to that there had been any trouble.

"What sort of trouble?"

"I don't know. Blackmail was my first thought. But almost anything. Still, I haven't found anything at all to worry about. And I've begun to think that maybe the burglary didn't mean anything after all. It's possible, isn't it, that there was a burglary, but they didn't find whatever it was they were after."

"That's always possible," Senator Farnsworth answered, dabbing at his thin lips with a paper napkin.

"I came to you for two reasons," I told him. "In the first place, I suppose I thought you might be one of the vulnerable people."

"Being in politics?"

"Exactly."

"No, not at all. I am not going anywhere. My seat is safe. And I don't care that much. In any event, I am letting it be known that I have had therapy, myself. It's a way of supporting the appropriation bill for mental health, of keeping the bill from turning into a party issue. It never was a secret. And I am using it publicly. So, you see, I have nothing at all to fear."

"I see . . ."

"But you said there was a second reason?"

"Yes," I said. "I just don't know what to think any more. Without any evidence one way or another, I have to trust my hunches. And I don't trust them very much. I don't have a whole lot of experience with this kind of thing. Crime, blackmail, whatever . . ."

"Ah, and you think I do?" Senator Farnsworth asked, smiling. For a man with such thin lips, he had a broad, warm smile.

"Well, you have a feel for public life. A different view of the way people work."

"I expect so. Sane deviousness, eh?"

I nodded.

"Well, first of all, I suppose I'm angry about it. The same way you must be. It's a very dirty thing to break into a psychiatrist's office. Still, we must be as objective as we can. None of your present patients has complained?"

"No."

"And no former patient has called you, come to see you, written . . ."

"No."

"Then there are two possibilities, aren't there?"

He paused, pleased with himself. I waited.

"Either the burglary did not produce what it was intended to produce, or it did, but with a patient who could not let you know that something had happened."

"All right. That's logical," I said. I was disappointed. Still, there was a show of satisfaction on the senator's face.

"You've been talking to some of your patients and former patients, the ones you thought were the likeliest targets?"

"That's right."

"That may have been a waste of time. If there were something for any of them to tell you, they'd have called you. A long time ago."

44

"Then to whom should I have been talking?"

"Survivors. Are any of your patients—your former patients, that is —deceased? I should think of that group first. Dead, or in prison somewhere, or out of the country. Any place where they couldn't have reached you if they wanted to."

I said nothing. I didn't have to. I felt a sinking feeling in my middle, not in the stomach where the popular phrase puts it, but near the diaphragm around the solar plexus. And it must have showed on my face.

"There are some deceased patients?"

"Two."

"I'd look there. Talk to their families, their friends, their business associates. Anything at all. What you want to find out is whether there was any trouble before they died, and if there was, whether there was any connection."

"Connection? You mean murder?"

"It's not out of the question, is it?"

"Nothing is. I don't even know what the question is any more. Gertrude Stein's last words: 'What was the answer? What was the question?' Forgive me, I'm babbling."

"We're all human, aren't we?" he said gently. "Look, if there is anything I can do for you, any doors you need opened, any cooperation from government, from the police . . ."

"I hope it doesn't come to that."

"So do I. But if it does, I have friends all over."

"It's nice to have friends," I said.

"You've helped me. I help you. That's politics, isn't it?"

"I'll let you know if I need anything," I promised.

"I hope you don't. Need anything, that is. But I'm here. Remember that."

"Thanks."

"Coffee?"

"No, no, thanks. I'd better be . . . getting to it."

"All right. You know where to find me."

I thanked him again and left.

It was still possible that nothing had happened. The dire possibilities that Senator Farnsworth had imagined were no more than that— possibilities. I had not been sufficiently imaginative, sufficiently logical. And the probability was not really changed by his having speculated as to what might have happened. In such ways I tried to cheer myself, tried to retain some objectivity and calm. It could still have happened exactly as I had supposed, with some amateurish break-in and no result at all. They had found nothing. There was no pressing reason to suppose otherwise, was there? There are not that many murders, are there? If there had been a murder, I'd have known about it, would have read about it in the papers, would have been called on by the police. These things are never so neat as they look in the movies. Surely, there are unsolved crimes, but those are most frequently the stupid, impulsive acts of violence for which there is no explanation, no motive, no sense. A mugging in which the victim falls the wrong way and splits his head open. But this? There would have to have been a most elaborate scenario, with the criminal or criminals breaking into my office and then killing. Did that make any sense? Did it feel right? Far-fetched, to say the very least.

Two dead patients. Dwayne French in an airplane crash. Easy to check that out, with the F.A.A. Or is it the C.A.B.? One of those government agencies. They look into all plane crashes, analyze wreckage, make reports. And the other? Adam Swett? A heart attack. Easy to check the medical records on that. In neither case, plane crash or heart attack, did it appear to be murder.

Consider a third possibility, that there was a break-in, that the burglars found something, that they were all set to blackmail or extort or coerce, or whatever it was they had planned to do . . . And then the victim died. Quite randomly and unconnectedly, died, frustrating them, ending the caper, whatever the caper was supposed to have been. Maybe it had never even got started. Which would be good reason for the family to have kept silent. They could not be expected to come and complain to me if there had been nothing to complain about. That felt rather better, rather more convincing.

I drove back through the traffic snarls feeling considerably better than I had as I'd left the senator's office. Traffic is a really interesting test of one's mood, a kind of gauge of one's tolerance to frustration. Boston and Cambridge traffic is, anyway. No great difference between one day's jams and those of the next, but one's patience and tolerance ebb and flow. I felt in control again, and . . . well, better. I could even leave the checking out of these two loose ends to Stanley. For my part, I supposed I would complete the Gestalt and check with the Kearns family, less out of any realistic concern than for the sake of completing the pattern of the list. And then I could get back to work.

Stanley was fine about it, couldn't have been better. "I'll go get you one of those deerstalker hats," he said. "Deer stalker or slayer. Anyway, one of those hats with the little brim in the front and the back. Like an old Studebaker. But I don't think you want to mess with a calabash pipe. Or morphine. Sherlock Holmes took morphine, didn't he?"

"Yes, I know. I feel silly about it, too. But how different is it, really, from psychiatry? Hints and clues and connections and conclusions. The process is close enough. Anyway, it's a comfortable theory," I said. "Even without the deerstalker hat, one can have theories. Either they got nothing, or they got something and the victim died, so that nothing happened. Nothing came of it."

"Then why did Elfinstone put it in the book?"

"I have no idea. I could invent something, but that's still another theory."

"All right, let me try," Stanley said, playing the student but also being the student. "Assume that you're right and that the victim died. Either Swett or French. There would still be some guilt, even if there weren't any cause for it. Or not at least legal guilt. The guy might feel that he'd done something terrible. And so he might put it down in a book as a way of confession. Is that it?"

"Something like it. Confession, or as a way of controlling the material. A writer might feel that, might try to fall back on what he knows best, what is most familiar to him, in order to digest the experience, to manage it. There must be a great feeling of power just in knowing that you can make the sentences come out any way you like. It might not have been anything quite so direct as a confession, but it works out to the same thing."

"Okay, I see that. That figures," Stanley said. "But you still want me to check out the C.A.B. and the City Hall. Boston and Cambridge, right?"

"Just to be sure."

"Today?"

"Today or tomorrow. No terrible rush about it. But it would be nice to get it . . . settled."

"I can see that. I'll get on it as soon as I can."

There were patients to see, and their problems to think about. With a clearer mind than I'd had in some days, I turned my attention to them. Or maybe it was just one of those lucky days. Connections all over the place. No huge insights maybe, but how often do they come along? Instead, small relationships of this kind of behavior to that incident, the discernment of a pattern, the understanding of what a patient was trying to say to himself and to the world. Small, satisfying, certain steps forward. There are doctors who disapprove of psychiatry as too theoretical, as a waste of medical training, as a nonsense. But there are days when the physical feeling of progress and improvement is as great as anything a surgeon can feel doing his cutting and sewing. And it was one of those days, exhilarating and exhausting.

I worked through until five, with patients, and then stayed at my desk to make notes until a little after six. I was just closing up shop and getting ready to relax with a Campari and soda and think about dinner, when the phone rang. It was Stanley.

"Just thought I'd call and let you know that we're halfway home. I checked out Swett. After all, he's the black man, right? Besides, the C.A.B. is across the river in Boston, and Swett's records were here in Central Square."

"And it's all right?"

"It's fine. The guy had a heart attack. No sweat, no Swett. All looking normal and reasonable. He dropped dead in a doctor's office. And the doctor signed the certificate. James Harney, M.D."

"Harney?"

"Yeah, anything wrong?"

"Yes," I said. "There is. Or there could be. I don't know. Any other name, and I'd be comfortable. But not this one."

"You know this doctor, Doctor?"

"No. Never met him. Don't know him. All I know about him is one thing. He's Elfinstone's doctor."

"That doesn't have to mean anything, does it?"

"It's a connection. It's a line. Sometimes that doesn't mean anything. Sometimes, as Freud said, a cigar is only a cigar. But it could mean . . ."

"You don't really believe it, do you?" he asked, trying to be helpful, to be comforting.

"I don't know. I need to look more. We're not home yet, to pick up on your phrase."

"Is there anything I can do? Tonight, I mean."

"No, thanks. I . . . I have to think a little. It's important for me to think. Besides, there's nothing that won't wait until tomorrow."

"I'll see you tomorrow, then."

He hung up. I put the phone back on its cradle as if it had bitten me.

No nice Campari and soda now. Campari and gin, half and half. And a long think.

Seven

All right, I thought, something happened. Was there a break-in? Yes. Without any question. Was there a connection between the break-in and Adam Swett? Yes, I was sure of it. Coincidence of that kind had to be significant. But signifying what?

The question, really, was whether to go to the police or not. Whether to go to the police yet. And if I did, what could I tell them? Show them the page in the book, and show them my office. And tell them that Greg Pitman was really Elfinstone, whose doctor signed the death certificate of one of my patients. "Go away, lady, you're nuts!"

Or, if they didn't say that, they'd think it, they'd tell me they'd look into it, and either forget about it or . . . Or mess it up. Put Elfinstone and Harney on their guard. It was not a lack of confidence in the police, but a lack of confidence in anyone who did not feel the way I did about there having to be something unpleasant hidden away there. Little wisps of perception and association floated through my consciousness. Doctors are tougher than other people about life and death, have to be, have been trained to be. Every intern learns when to give up, when to unplug the machines, when to stop the medication or increase it to lethal doses. Nobody talks about this much, and yet everyone knows about it. Not only doctors but laymen. There comes a point when there is nothing left but pain, unbearable pain for the patient, and pain and hideous expense for the patient's family. Unplug! End it! Out of simple charity, out of kindness, out of mercy. We learn this, or most of us do, and we also learn a soldierly toughness, in order to survive, ourselves. All the terrible intern jokes are devices for putting distance between ourselves and the sufferings of those around us. And sometimes there is a feeling of great power, of omnipotent wisdom, which would be clinical if it were not socially useful and necessary. A lot of doctors could wind up in mental wards if they were judged on standards that society applies to accountants, lumberjacks, realtors, salespeople . . .

Without deciding that he was guilty of anything, without having any idea yet about what exactly he might have done, I knew that Harney was capable of a great deal. Any doctor is. And that had to weigh in my considerations. But explain that to the police?

No, I couldn't believe it. I couldn't imagine it, really. In order to save embarrassment, we will go to very great lengths indeed. I had to go ahead a little further, at least to get enough information together to make a plausible presentation when I did go to the police. Senator Farnsworth had offered his help, but the very kindness of his offer made it a matter of delicacy and tact as to how far I ought to impose. I had my suspicions, my hunches . . . The thing to do was to pursue them a little further, to go the next step or two. And then, in the ripeness of time, to go to the authorities.

Soothed by the reasonableness of that scenario, I poured myself another drink. I thought of making dinner, but did not have either the energy or the desire. A piece of cheese, a piece of fruit, and I was satisfied. Sated. I went to bed early, and slept like a baby.

But the next day the questions returned. Or had turned into a new question. How to go ahead, how to get this further information that I needed in order to have something reasonable to say to the police? I let it hang through the morning at the clinic, and then popped it to Stanley. I wasn't putting the burden of the decision on his shoulders, but I needed someone to talk to, to react against, in order to find out what I thought, myself.

"My impulse," I confessed, "is to go to Harney. Just go. Look at him. Talk to him. Maybe I'm imagining all this."

"You don't want to do that," Stanley said.

"Well, I have mixed feelings."

"You don't know what to ask him yet."

"I wasn't thinking of asking him anything. I thought I'd just turn up. As a patient."

"A psychiatrist patient?"

"Just a patient," I said. "I don't look like a psychiatrist. Who does?"

"Freud did."

"I always thought he looked like a banker. Or a shipowner."

"Okay. Let's say you show up as a patient. He shoots you full of stuff. How does that help you?"

"As I said. I get to see him. To listen to him."

"Better off going the long way round. Save him for later. See Mrs. Swett first."

"I suppose you're right."

"It bothers you to see her? You think you failed her husband? You feel guilty about it? Garbage!"

"A little of that, maybe."

"You didn't break in here, did you?"

"No."

"Well, okay, then."

"Well," I echoed, "okay, then."

And I looked up Swett's number, called, got Mrs. Swett, and made an appointment to see her that evening. At her home. She gave me the address, in Brighton, and told me how to get there. I had not asked. She had merely assumed I needed instructions. Considerate? Or defiant? A black neighborhood? Or a mixed? A place, at any rate, where my sort would need instructions to get to? A drawing of lines, perhaps, and a setting-out of the terms of our meeting? Those were the questions that rose in my mind as I hung up. There were, of course, ways of dismissing them, or at least other questions to contradict and neutralize the first set. Was I being touchy and supersensitive? Had the fault—if it was a fault—been hers or mine? Still, they persisted.

The answers came that evening. The directions were useful, after all, because there was a tangle of one-way streets and peculiar bends. Still, with a map which I keep in my glove compartment, and having only a vague sense of direction, I could have found the place. A respectable middle-class neighborhood, with neat lawns looking all the more appealing because they were small. Useless picket fences, two feet high, marked out the property lines. The area had been developed thirty or thirty-five years ago. The way to tell is by looking at the trees on the lawns. Guess their age and you know the age of the neighborhood. In the late dusk of daylight-saving time the houses on the block seemed snug and secure.

To me. To a black man from Detroit they might have appeared rather different. A paradise? A challenge? It would have depended, perhaps, on how the neighborhood accepted him. Out in the street, sitting behind the wheel of the car, I had the odd notion that the houses were the neighborhood, that they sat there like great boxy beasts, conferring with one another in mysterious ways, and accepting the comings and goings of the humans as . . . as sharks accept the comings and goings of pilot fish. Huge, quiet monsters, they were obviously related, had survived together for a long while, managing pretty well. Had Adam Swett perceived them to be friendly or hostile?

The neighbors might have worried about their property values. Or they might have felt a little intimidated by his position as a dean at Harvard. Or, more probably, both. In which case, there might have been little interchange between them and him. But that might have been welcome on both sides. Coming, as he did, from a poor, urban childhood, the dream would have included privacy, even the exaggerated privacy of semi-ostracism. He might have thought all whites were like that? No, not a Harvard dean.

I got out of the car, walked up the walk between a pair of healthy-looking hydrangeas, and rang the bell. Mrs. Swett appeared, a small, trim, coffee-colored woman with very delicate, rather Caucasian features. A less theatrical Lena Horne. She invited me inside.

A quick look around, and I was entirely confused. All my expectations had been irrelevant. This was a woman like me, with the same standards, the same tastes, the same badges of caste and class. The taste is harder to come by than the money to afford it. In fact, the Cambridge academic style is rather simple. Workbench, and Door Store, with accents of Design Research and Upper Story, and a few old things one has inherited or somehow elected to love. A simple, almost a Spartan purity of line. I realized, with a pang, that I had expected something . . . well, a little showier, a little more recognizably black. But then, I had known only Adam Swett and had been guessing from him. He had, evidently, married upwards.

We introduced ourselves—her name was Lila—and she offered me coffee, which I accepted, wondering whether it had always been Lila, or whether Delilah had got itself shortened down to something more manageable.

"Black or white?" Mrs. Swett asked, returning with the coffee.

"I beg your pardon?"

"Your coffee? With cream?"

"Please," I said. It was not beginning well.

"Sugar?"

"No, thank you."

She handed me the cup, prepared one for herself, and sat down across the slatted coffee table. She took a sip of coffee and then, without saying anything, raised her eyebrows slightly, asking, unmistakably, what I wanted to talk about, why I had asked to see her, why I had come.

I told her. No leading up to it, nor beating about any bushes, but straight out. How there was evidence that my files had been invaded some time ago, and how I was concerned for my patients.

She understood that. She was, herself, in social work administration. A competent woman. We could be businesslike about things. Fine.

"The worst fear," I said, "is blackmail. Or even worse than that, I suppose, blackmail which might have led to . . ."

"Murder?" she asked. "Or suicide?"

"Either one."

"Adam died of natural causes. A heart attack."

"Yes, I know. But it's possible that someone had approached him . . . I mean, it's logically possible."

"I understand," she said, "but I don't think so. There isn't anything Adam could have been blackmailed about."

"Still, you can understand my concern. It's a delicate situation. I have to ask these questions. I don't intend any reflection at all . . ."

"No, of course not," she said. Too sharply? Or was it only her manner? I wished that the talk had begun differently, that I had some range to judge from.

"He had been depressed," I said, trying to go back a little, not only in time but in the tone of our present conversation.

"Yes, for a time. He had certain kinds of pressures . . . Which of us does not? He worked through them pretty well."

"We didn't get very far," I told her. "I saw your husband three times. He withdrew from treatment."

"He was too busy for it," Mrs. Swett said defiantly. And then, more gently, "At least he thought he was. It was a bad year. He just didn't have the time. He went to pieces at the end of the term."

"He went elsewhere?"

"Yes. And felt much better. For a while. For six months or so. And then he went into a hospital for a couple of weeks."

"What hospital?"

"A private hospital in New Haven. The Herndon Clinic."

"Why New Haven?"

"He was in New Haven for a conference. Some meeting at Yale. And something happened to him. He was there for two weeks. Maybe a little more. And when he came out, he was all right. He really was."

"But before that? Before he went to New Haven, he was seeing someone here?"

"Yes."

"Whom was he seeing?" I asked.

"Dr. Harney."

"And there was no pressure of any kind? No blackmail?"

"From Dr. Harney?"

"From anyone."

"What would they blackmail him about?"

"I know about his life in Detroit, when he was younger. I . . . I don't like to bring this all up, but I have to. It's possible, isn't it?"

"Nobody knew about any of that."

"I did."

"It was in your files?"

"No, not really, not in any way that anyone could figure out. I have very sketchy notes, sometimes. *Aides mémoires*. But he did tell me."

"I don't think he would have told Dr. Harney. That wouldn't have been necessary."

"Were things all right here? Toward the end, I mean. Was he unhappy?"

"It was difficult for him. He had some troubles. Mostly Harvard's troubles, but his own, too. He didn't know who he was any more. It was hard for him. My father was a doctor, and my mother was a schoolteacher. It was different for me. I . . ."

She stopped, took another sip of coffee, used the time to size me up, to consider her own intuitions. Apparently one of us passed the test.

"He was my city dude! It was a nice, clear thing for a long time. But it made him awfully ambitious. He wanted to please me. He tried very hard. Maybe he tried too hard. Maybe all that trying, maybe it killed him."

"If that was how it happened, then that's all right, isn't it?" I offered.

"Is it?" she asked sharply.

"No," I agreed. "It's never all right."

"No, it isn't."

"Was he drinking?" I asked. "Sleeping a lot?"

"No, nothing like that."

The next question would have been whether there were women, other women. But I hadn't the heart.

"He worked a lot?" I asked.

"All the time."

"It could have been overwork, then?"

"What else?"

"I don't know. I . . . I haven't any reason to think otherwise. I came to ask whether you do."

She shook her head no.

"I'm sorry to have had to bother you, Mrs. Swett."

"No, no. I understand. You have to do this. It's the right thing."

I reached out and touched her hand. Then I left.

Outside, behind the wheel, I looked at those houses again. It was darker now, but they seemed more menacing than before, beasts that had chewed Adam Swett to little pieces and spat him out.

Or had they?

The next morning I called the Herndon Clinic in New Haven. I made an appointment to go down there and see them. Saturday morning.

Eight

All right? Satisfied? Ready to let it go? I asked myself these questions in rather a vexed mood, annoyed at myself for what I knew to be willful obstinacy. It had not been a very satisfactory talk, perhaps, and yet the woman had been clear enough, and reliable enough. I had not been able to get close to her, but then I hadn't needed to. She was obviously competent, reasonable, shrewd. She had said that there was nothing, had been no blackmail attempts. And I believed her. Why this insane trip to New Haven, then? Three hours driving, or a little more, each way. Six hours! A whole day shot to blazes! For what?

I mean, honestly! What the hell did I think I was doing? Gathering evidence to take to the police? Yes, it sounds plausible enough. One has read such sentences in mysteries, in stupid books by people like Elfinstone, but one doesn't do such things. We learn in modern urban living not to get involved, to step over bodies in the street. Not just your ordinary laymen, either, but doctors who don't want to get involved in malpractice suits. It's mean, perhaps, but it's self-preservation, and one ignores self-preservation at one's peril.

I didn't want to go to New Haven. I wanted to spend the day walking around Newberry Street, looking at pictures. I wanted to spend the night with Martin. I had errands to do, a dress at the cleaner's being invisibly woven where I'd snagged it and made a little triangular tear. I had to take my suede jacket into a furrier to get the pocket restitched where it had come loose. I didn't have to go to New Haven!

For whom? Assume that Adam Swett had been the victim of something. There was no way to help him now. Dead people do not need medical attention, or, indeed, attention of any kind. Pebbles on their graves, perhaps—which Reich thinks may be symbolic stones to prevent their ghosts from coming back to haunt us. But no help I could give. And Mrs. Swett, Lila, did not need my help, or want it. Arrogance, sheer arrogance! And if it wasn't Swett? Then, clearly, I was wasting my time. And energy and gas.

As if to prove to myself that I had been ridiculous, or perhaps with a hope that something else might turn up, some distraction, some excuse not to go all the way to New Haven, I called the Kearns family. I invented some cock-and-bull story about a statistical inquiry to which I was responding, and I asked a lot of questions about Patricia, among which were the relevant ones. Had there been any pressure from peers, from family friends, from anyone at all, having anything to do with the fact that she had been in therapy? No, nothing like that. Had there been any change in external conditions of living? No, none. Had there been any disadvantages that had presented themselves that had not been related to the therapy, any reversals of any other kind? No, knock wood.

I said I was glad to hear it, and glad of the excuse to call and talk with Mrs. Kearns. I asked, rather more informally and directly, how they had all been. And I was told, quite warmly and directly, that they were fine, that Patricia was doing well, would be in to see me when she got home from school . . .

There was nothing there. I hadn't really expected anything. After all, the logic of Senator Farnsworth's observation was still good. Anybody with problems would have been in touch with me. Anybody who couldn't get in touch was the possible subject of real concern. And that narrowed the list to Swett and to Dwayne French. Still, just to complete my list, to cross off the last of the names, I had called Mrs. Kearns.

Dwayne French had not married. He had a sister. I found her name in my files and called her. Could she see me? Yes. This afternoon? Yes, she could manage that. Would five-thirty be inconvenient? No, that would be fine, she could work that. I thanked her. Lewisburg Square. Not very far away from Elfinstone, actually, but then a lot of people live on Beacon Hill. You get that in residential areas, don't you? Of course you do. It isn't significant. There are, after all, coincidences.

After my last patient, then, I had another brief talk with Stanley, told him what had happened, and what was about to happen. I had got nothing from Mrs. Swett. I was going to see Mrs. Jarman, Dwayne French's sister. I expected nothing from her, either.

"Then why do it?"

"A couple of days ago I could have answered that. I could have said all kinds of intelligent, admirable things. I could have told you that one can't just do nothing, that one must at least try. But today, I don't know. Inertia more than anything."

"Friction will overcome that," he said.

"Yes, I suppose that's what I'm hoping. I begin to feel that I'm being rather foolish."

"Would you feel worse the other way? If you stopped?"

"I'm trying to decide that."

"Let me know how it comes out."

So I went over to Lewisburg Square. No place to park over there, usually, and I took the MBTA to Charles and walked, or trudged, rather, up those mad streets. Found the apartment and rang. The exertion of the trip, the crush in the subway at that time of day, and the final insult of the hill to climb had been enough to make me decide that I *was* being ridiculous. That this was it. This, and then, peculiarly, New Haven—but only because I had called and had made the appointment. But after that, nothing. Finished. I gave up.

The bell rang back, admitting me, and I went inside and up a flight of stairs. A better building than Elfinstone's, and yet it was sad in the same way. This, too, had once been a grand private house and now was chopped up into little apartments for childless couples, bachelors, widows. Mrs. Jarman greeted me and invited me in. I refused the offer of a cup of tea, sat down, and did the bit. I explained about the break-in, the suspicion I'd had that one of my patients might have been compromised, and came round, at last, to asking her about her brother.

"There was some trouble," Mrs. Jarman said. "Some business about some stock transfers. A technicality, I believe, but Dwayne was awfully worried about it. But I don't see how that could connect . . ."

"With the accident?" I asked.

"No, of course not. I meant with your files. He didn't talk about business with you, did he? That's not what people talk about to doctors. Even to psychiatrists . . . Is it?"

"No," I said truthfully. "I didn't know anything about it."

She relaxed, visibly. Odd. Had there been some irregularity? Had she been part of it?

"Of course, it's possible that someone might have been looking for something that wasn't there . . ."

"But if they were looking for something that wasn't there, they didn't find it, did they?"

"That would follow," I said, wondering still. She seemed very cheerful about her peculiar theorem. She was a delicate, birdlike lady with very precise features and half-glasses that made her look schoolteacherish. She seemed to be a whole generation older than her brother, but a lot of that was a matter of effect. Eight or nine years, perhaps. But she played for it, worked at it. Actually tried to look as old as she could. Interesting.

"Do you know about any pressure that might have been put on him? Other than by the situation itself, I mean," I asked. "By the authorities . . . ?"

"None that he mentioned to me. Of course, that doesn't mean anything, does it? He didn't always tell me everything."

From the way she said it, I rather thought that perhaps he did. But that was none of my business, or I didn't think it was. Not this business.

"Are you sure you wouldn't like a little tea?" Mrs. Jarman asked. "I would."

"If it's no trouble."

"No trouble. If you're making one cup, there's no trouble to make two. Less, really. One cup, I usually make in the cup with a tea bag. Two, I'd make with a pot. It tastes better. Wasteful for just one person, but it tastes better. You're doing me a favor, don't you see?"

"I shouldn't have refused in the first place."

She smiled at me, congratulating, approving. Odd woman, I thought. I couldn't quite make it out. She had, it seemed, some secret, something to hide. And yet she was so strenuously friendly, within the confines of the persona of age and gentility she had put on. Lila Swett had been more hostile, more fearful. What did that mean? A worse secret? Or a different way of dealing with its concealment.

She made the tea. We drank it, and she tried to reassure me. "Even if there had been something . . . something embarrassing, which is possible, nothing could have come of it. It was a plane crash. A commercial airline. Sixty-four people were killed. It couldn't possibly tie in, could it?"

"I don't see how."

"So there's nothing for you to worry about. Not on poor Dwayne's account, at any rate."

"No," I said.

"But with someone else?"

"I'm not sure."

"You don't seem . . . how shall I say? Relieved."

"No, I don't suppose I am."

"It isn't your fault. It couldn't have been. You can't be responsible for a burglary."

"No, in a way I can't. But I am."

"Yes, I see that. It's how I think I would feel. How I hope I would feel. You will be careful, won't you?"

I promised I would.

So different, so entirely different from Mrs. Swett!

Back home, I continued the old argument, but in new terms. The way the question now stood, it was whether to go to New Haven or not. A wasted day? But I didn't believe that, not any more. I realized that there was a difference between Mrs. Jarman and Mrs. Swett that was not just a matter of manner and style. Mrs. Jarman had been pleasant and gracious and warm, but beyond that, she had nothing to hide, was willing to put herself a little bit into my situation, to extend herself. She could afford to extend herself because she had nothing to hide. Mrs. Swett? Well, there might be other reasons, but she had refused to recognize even that the nature of my inquiry was kindly, was concerned. It had, somehow, threatened her.

That was not, in my specialty, anything new. On the contrary, I had to deal with it all the time. And I was certainly able to recognize withdrawal, resistance, and fear when I saw it. For what reason, and whether it was relevant to my questions, I could not begin to guess. But it was noted, and in a professional way I had to deal with it. At least look a little further. So, to the clinic . . .

But the energy it would take. The driving, particularly. All that way, alone in the car, pushing the damned thing down those tiresome four-lane monster roads. I didn't like the idea very much. I thought perhaps of taking a train.

Okay, when are the trains? I called 1-800-555-1212 and got Amtrak information, and wrote down the number. Then I called Amtrak —God knows where they actually are—and got a recording saying that all the circuits were busy and asking me to try again in a few minutes. So I poured myself a Campari and called again, and got the recording again. Shit! I called the operator and told her that I kept getting this recording about how the circuits were all busy. I asked her to try it for me, and I got through—to another recording, this one saying that all the agents were busy, and advising me that calls would be treated sequentially. "Treated sequentially," for God's sake. I didn't want to be treated any way but humanly, humanely. And yet, I was determined to get through to a human voice, to find out at least what the times were of departures and arrivals, to break through the barricades of recorded messages and . . .

But that was exactly what I was doing, wasn't it? It had very little to do with Adam Swett, or even with Charles Elfinstone or the bad doctor Harney. It was a matter of completing the pattern, of interpreting resistance as challenge, of accepting the challenge, of overcoming it. The standard personality configuration of an eldest child, an older female with younger male siblings, a middle-class, upwardly mobile family . . . I knew all that, but it didn't make it any different or any less true. I hung on grimly, waiting, sipping at my Campari, refusing to accept defeat, and finally I got yet another recording which thanked me for waiting and promised once more that all calls would be treated sequentially. Was that supposed to make me feel better, knowing that everyone was suffering as much as I? If they treated calls randomly, then at least one could hope for luck, for something. How very gray and grim this was!

An agent came on the line at last, and was perfectly nice. He told me when the trains were, offered me a turbo-train at 9:10 A.M. that arrived at 11:58. And there was a return turbo at 5:48, arriving at South Station at 8:35. So the evening would not necessarily be lost. I would not be exhausted from driving. I could see Martin, or a movie, or maybe both. I thanked the Amtrak agent, hung up, and settled for the train. It was still probably stupid, but at least I could read on the way down and the way back, and get caught up on some homework I'd neglected because of this ridiculous business.

I picked up the phone to call Martin, and then hesitated. Was it perhaps unfair to use him this way? He was a dear man, but in some ways confused. Or romantic. Or anyway, too serious. There is an Auden line, somewhere, about how, "If equal affection cannot be/ Let the more loving one be me." The other way, it is rather a responsibility. One dislikes to hurt people. And yet I knew it would be

62

more hurtful not to call, not to see him. Not to sleep with him. And if Auden was correct, he did not have such a bad deal after all. For my own part, I needed the companionship, the company. Psychiatrists are rather cut off, as most doctors are not—they get to talk with one another, scrubbing up for operations, or over coffee after rounds in the hospital. That's probably why I took on the work at the clinic. Or part of the reason. To feel connections, to be part of a staff, of an institution. To have people to talk to. And yet, my life was so busy that I had very little chance. At night it was different, and the need was greater. But there were other conflicting needs.

Thinking about this in a random way, not treating it sequentially or anything so gross, I decided that I might as well call, and did. And got no answer. And regretted . . . Calling? Or getting no answer? As the girl in *Take the Money and Run* said, "Go know!"

I sat there like a dummy, looking at the phone. Whom did I want to call? There are moods like that, and people have them often enough. A wish to make some connection. But if not with Martin, then with whom? I was beginning to shred!

No, I wasn't. It took a while, and a little luck, but by asking myself whom I wanted to call, I had got through the worst of it. And had found, almost incidentally, the answer. New Haven? I could go there or not. And it was probably sensible to go. It was more than possible that I'd find out something useful.

Still, the man I wanted to see, the man I wanted to talk to, was Dr. Harney. Stanley's warning notwithstanding. Or perhaps because of Stanley's warning.

The question, I told Felicity, was how to manage it.

And that, I promised myself, rather cheerfully, I would sleep on.

Nine

The Herndon Clinic is just outside of New Haven in one of those ugly old buildings that got built in the boom just after the Civil War when New Haven supplied gunpowder and munitions for most of the Union troops. It was first a mansion, and then a school, and then a retreat for some order of nuns, and then, finally, a clinic. Ralph Herndon still runs it. He and his brother John started it in the fifties as a drug and amphetamine center, but it changed over the years to a psychiatric emphasis. Not so much of a change, really, but it was an interesting history. And it was interesting, too, that Adam Swett should have just happened to be in New Haven when he collapsed, that of all the places in New Haven, and there are several very good ones, he should have arrived at Herndon.

There were all sorts of reasonable explanations, of course. There are conferences all the time, and for Dean Swett to have been in New Haven was not peculiar at all. For him to have wanted a place that was reliable and yet discreet, or for his friends in New Haven to assume that he would have wanted such a thing . . . Well, it could have happened that way. All psychiatric clinics and hospitals are supposed to be discreet, and mostly they are, of course. But in academics, word does get around. The academic grapevine is a particularly tight one, and a word, an inadvertent reference at a dinner party can set it all humming. So it was, in ways, a convenient and reasonable choice. Still, the development of the place as a drug treatment center, and from there, when the drug thing leveled off, into a more general psychiatric clinic did seem to dovetail into Swett's life—or into what I was beginning to assume about Swett's life.

I arrived at the clinic with a very nervous cabdriver who assumed that I was a patient and was evidently expecting me to become violent at any minute. A very apprehensive man, and therefore extremely polite. No chatter at all on the ride from the sad derelict of a railroad station out toward West Haven, a diffident inquiry about whether I would mind the radio, and a most respectful delivery at the door of the clinic. He actually got out of the cab and opened the door for me. A quick flash: If the pressures of modern living increase so that even more people are just barely sub-clinical but mostly crazy, will public manners improve?

I paid the taxi driver, smiled at him, thanked him in a way that was sufficiently grave and formal as to appear, perhaps, half mad —I didn't want to disappoint him—and went inside. Dr. Herndon was expecting me, and I was shown at once into a rather homey conference room. Either Herndon, or his wife, or perhaps his decorator, had done it to look like a comfortable living room with Victorian and Edwardian warmth. There was a Biedermeyer table at one end, looking a little out of place, but that helped. It looked as though the room had more or less happened, as rooms in homes sometimes do. Unlikely in this instance, but . . . comforting. And supportive for the families of patients come to hope for the best and afraid of hearing the worst. Dr. Herndon, a slight, gray-haired, very New Englandy man with a habit of raising his eyebrows as if he were startled—but pleasantly startled—came into the room and welcomed me. With an efficiency that was perfectly reasonable and graceful, he asked whether my trip had been pleasant, whether I wanted coffee, and what he could do for me.

I had given considerable thought, sitting in the train, to the best way to begin. I wanted to communicate my concern, and yet not to appear paranoid. On the other hand, there was very little I could say that was able to stand by itself without interpretations and the gloss of mood and intuition. I began by telling him about my conversation with Senator Farnsworth, and how it had been the senator's idea that I should look into the histories of recent patients who had died. And from there I worked backwards to the burglary and the way I'd discovered it.

"I take it, then, that one of your patients was also one of our patients?"

"I'm interested in Adam Swett."

"He's dead?"

"A year ago, nearly."

"I see," Dr. Herndon said. And then, "I thought it was Swett you were going to ask about."

"Oh?"

"Partly it was the geography of it. Cambridge and all. But part of it was spontaneous. I thought of him."

"What can you tell me about him?" I asked.

"I can get the file. We can look at it together," he offered. "I'll be back in a few moments. You sure you won't have some coffee?"

"No, no, thank you," I said.

He was gone for a longer time than I had expected. I thought at first he would step out and then be back in a minute or two. Then, as the time stretched out, I supposed that he was rummaging around in some dead-file storeroom, or waiting while somebody else rummaged. Then I began to wonder if perhaps the Herndon Clinic might also have been burgled, whether the same people who had broken into my office might have come here and snatched the file. Of course, they hadn't taken any of my files, but there were explanations for that. Assume that my files didn't have what they were looking for—or worried about. And assume that the Herndon files did. They would not necessarily be inconsistent to take his and not mine, to use them or to destroy them. The possibility that had popped into my head seemed to turn into a probability, even into a certainty as the interval turned into a quarter of an hour.

He returned, and I looked to see the shock on his face. No shock. No profusion of apologies. Instead, he sat down and said, "Now, Dr. Chayse, you have some identification? Something that suggests who you are?"

I showed him my driver's license, my ID from the clinic, my American Express card.

"You understand," he said, "that anyone can come in here and claim to be . . . anyone."

"Of course."

"I called Mrs. Swett. It took me longer to get through to her than I'd expected. She tells me you were Adam Swett's doctor, but only briefly . . ." He raised his eyebrows in interrogation.

"That's right," I said. "He withdrew from treatment. I saw him only two—or perhaps three—times. Still, his name was in my files. The files apparently were broken into."

"Mrs. Swett tells me he died of a heart attack."

"That is what the death certificate says."

"Have you any reason to doubt it?" Dr. Herndon asked.

"Nothing concrete. But . . . Was he examined while he was here? I mean, a physical examination?"

"Of course."

"Was there any indication of any heart trouble?"

"No, none. On the other hand, he had been using amphetamines rather heavily."

"Did he know that?"

"He denied knowing anything about it, actually."

"Didn't that seem curious to you?"

"One is never quite sure how to take these explanations, professions, apologies, justifications . . . Whether to believe them or not. There is a degree of paranoia associated with amphetamine psychosis . . ."

"Of course," I agreed. "But sometimes even paranoids have real enemies."

"That's always possible, isn't it?" Dr. Herndon replied. "He claimed to have been under treatment in Boston. Vitamins, or some such rubbish."

"The same doctor was the one who signed the death certificate."

Herndon looked away, gazed for a moment through the window and out to a green lawn. "It's a very delicate business, this. Assuming that what you are implying may have in fact happened, it's quite another thing to prove it. And unless proven, it could be very messy."

"What do I do, then, forget it?"

"I don't know all the circumstances. I'm not sure I could advise you even if I did. But how is any of this tied into the burglary? Or is it?"

"I think it may be. If there is anything at all to what I've been supposing."

"You're not sure that there is?"

"No, I'm not sure of anything."

"Then let it go. If you can, let it go. There is nothing you can gain, and there is great risk, great risk."

"How was he when he left here?" I asked, only apparently changing the subject.

"Clean. He was off the amphetamines, and he'd rested a lot and eaten a lot. He was better. And he seemed to be quite stable, mentally. Stable as most people walking around, certainly."

"And he went back to Cambridge, and then died."

"It could have happened that way. He could have died just like that. Or there might have been new pressures, or a recurrence of old pressures. He might have gone back to this doctor of his, and gone back to these *vitamins* . . . And they can kill people. It could have been something like that."

"Do you think that's likely?"

"I don't know what's likely and what isn't. I do know that a lot of people are more than likely to do very unlikely things from time to time. As he may have done."

"Well, as I say, I'm not sure of anything. But it seems very odd. And I don't very much like the idea of having my files broken into."

"I quite agree with you there," Herndon said. "But Mrs. Swett didn't seem very—how shall I say?—enthusiastic. She didn't seem enthusiastic at all about your inquiries."

"And doesn't that seem odd?"

"Perhaps, but there may be reasons. One has no idea what she may not want known. He may have behaved badly in ways that have nothing to do with the rest of this. If there is any rest of this."

"That's possible," I agreed. "But you say that his heart was good, and his physical condition seemed . . . sound?"

He thought for a moment, and then left the room again. He returned after only a matter of seconds with a manila file in his hand. He offered it to me. The physical examination had been noted on the first page. Blood pressure was normal. Cholesterol count was admirably low. I scanned the results of a fairly complete series of tests.

"For a man on amphetamines, he was quite healthy," Dr. Herndon said.

"And he claimed not to know that he had been on amphetamines?"

"So he claimed."

"Is there anything else that might be helpful to me?" I asked. "Not for my conclusions, but for my decision really as to whether to drop it. Anything you think I ought to know that fits, or that surprises by not fitting?"

"He talked," Herndon said, "a lot about Nietzsche."

"About what?"

"About Nietzsche. In therapy. I mention it because you asked for things that surprised by not fitting. It remains in my mind. Nothing useful, perhaps, but I remember it. Otherwise, there's very little . . ."

"Well, you've been very helpful. I wish I felt better about all this. One way or another, I'm sure I shall."

"It may just go away. Disappear," Herndon said. "He did."

"Yes, he did, didn't he?"

Dr. Herndon got up. I got up, thanked him once more, and went out to the receptionist to ask her to call me a taxi.

I had four hours on the trip back in which to think. I had work with me, papers to read, notes to look at. And yet I never even thought of opening my wicker-work briefcase. Instead, I tried to imagine what Adam Swett's life must have been like. Surely he had come out of the Herndon Clinic on some random day, had called in the same way for a taxi, had been driven to the railroad station, had waited for a train, and then had waited while the train rumbled along the old tracks taking him home. He would have felt—joy? No, I could not believe that. It was not a matter of my own failure to like Lila Swett. It was a coldness in her, a sacrifice she had made, or had been forced to make, a very long time ago, in order to become what her parents wanted her to be, what she herself wanted to be, what the world demanded that she be. It had cost her dearly, and although one might admire her, one could not feel much warmth toward her. One could not even imagine Adam Swett feeling much warmth. Pride, maybe, and a sense of achievement, just from the idea that he was good enough for her, had won her, had been able to survive with her. But not the kind of comfort an overworked, fragile man would need. And that was interesting. After all, had not Dr. Herndon speculated that there might be other kinds of misbehavior that Mrs. Swett did not want known?

Another woman, perhaps? Younger, probably, and less demanding? Admiring him for what he was, and giving him the uncritical acceptance he must have needed? There was no evidence for it, but it seemed to be a plausible kind of question.

There were other ways to imagine reasons for Mrs. Swett's reluctance to have me nosing around. But the other ways were all more sinister. She had known about Dr. Harney. She could not possibly have approved of Dr. Harney. It was not inconceivable that she had arranged the business with the Herndon Clinic, that she had been responsible for Adam's going to New Haven and his going from the meeting directly to the clinic. Out of fear of Harney? As a way of getting Adam away from Harney? Something of that kind. And Harney might have had some bludgeon, might still have one . . .

That was the worst I could imagine. And I was not certain that I believed it or trusted it. More conservative guesses, more banal situations seem to recommend themselves sometimes. So, imagine a mistress. Let her resent the hell out of the mistress, and let her even be irrational enough not to want to share the dead Adam Swett with any mistress. I could see that. The unbending it would take for her to tell me that there was a girl I might talk to . . .

White? Or black? Terrible for her, either way. Young, or not so young? Again, terrible for Lila Swett, whichever it had been.

Or, then again, there was no logic that excluded both possibilities. They could perfectly well coexist. A mistress and some connection with Harney.

Lila Swett was alive, had rights, had legitimate interests in this, as I did not. And Adam Swett was dead. Drop it? Without any question, that was what Dr. Herndon had been trying to urge me to do.

All I needed was an excuse, a way out. And I knew I would take it.

Ten

We were in bed. We were lying there talking, feeling good, feeling relaxed the way people sometimes do after making love. The radio was playing Mahler songs, and their languid, liquid extravagance was quite welcome. And then the phone rang.

"I'm not here," Martin said, making a joke of it.

I picked it up on the second ring. It was John, calling from Denver. Just to say hello. To let me know about a meeting in Atlanta he was thinking about, wondering whether to go, whether I might go.

Martin lay back in the bed, patient, waiting, poor dear. But then, I had had no idea that John would call, couldn't have expected it. On the other hand, there was John, feeling lonely, feeling like talking. What was there to do? I talked to him.

Martin reached over and touched me. As if there were no telephone conversation, he started to stroke me with his fingertips. His eyes were closed. It was funny, really, and so wonderfully simple. I closed my eyes as well, and listened to John and felt Martin's fingertips touching me . . .

It must have lasted five minutes, perhaps a little more. Then John rang off. And Martin opened his eyes.

"That's terrible," he said. "Women!"

"What's terrible?" I asked him.

"Talking to him, and being here with me."

"What was I to do?" I asked. "If I'd been short with him, if I'd tried to disengage, then he'd have known . . ."

"That's the worst part of it," Martin answered, groaning. "You were right. By any sane standard, you were perfectly right. It's just that it's still terrible."

"Or nice," I said. "You aren't jealous, are you?"

"No, but then, I'm here. The idea of it is what's terrible. I'll never be able to talk to you on the telephone again . . ."

"Yes, you will."

"I know. I will, but it won't be the same. It's crazy."

"Is it?"

"It is, it is," he said. "Of course, I could always ask if you're listening to Mahler. Some code thing like that. That way, you could let me know . . ."

"Would you want to know?"

"No."

"Well, there you are."

"Thanks," he said, rolling over and burying his face in the pillow.

I was sorry he felt that way, sorry he had been hurt. I couldn't be sorry for what I had done, but to have handled the phone call any other way would have meant hurting two people rather than one. And the one had no particular cause to feel injury. It was not, after all, a surprise. Men do get themselves into the most uncomfortable positions sometimes, I thought, while women are more . . . well, calm.

And then I thought of Mrs. Swett, and wondered about her attitude. Assume that there had been a mistress, some young girl perhaps. That still would not account for the reserve, the hostility . . .

"Martin?"

"What?"

"I went to New Haven today. To the Herndon Clinic."

"You're changing the subject."

"I hadn't thought there was anything else to say about it. I'm going on to another subject, if that's all right?"

"Oh God, I suppose. Sure, why not, let's," he said, rolling back over.

I told him about the records at the Herndon Clinic, and about my uneasy feelings about the death certificate that Dr. Harney had signed. I told him about Harney being Elfinstone's doctor. I told him about Mrs. Swett and the way in which she had resisted me, almost as if she was afraid of me.

"Well?" he asked.

"Well, something's wrong. Don't you feel it? There's something peculiar about it."

"Drop it. For her sake, Mrs. Swett's, I mean. And for your own sake. If it's funny, it could be dangerous. There's nothing obliging you to stir up trouble, is there?"

"He came to me for help."

"Oh, come on, don't give me any Dr. Kildare crap. All kinds of people come to us all the time, and we do what we can for them. This guy is dead, remember? You're not going to help him. And she doesn't want your help. And I don't like your messing around with this."

"You don't like it?"

"I don't like it. Look, I know I don't have any rights. I can't tell you what to do. But I was thinking there, a while back, when you were on the telephone, about how it used to be in Japan. I did my army time in Japan. And one of the big turn-ons was listening to other people through the paper walls. In the whorehouses. You could go down there just for drinks, and sit and listen. Or you'd tell yourself that that was what you were going to do. But it was a wild thing. And then, just now, with you, I thought that this ought to be a big turn-on too, you know? Except that it wasn't. It wasn't. I care about you too much. I get jealous. I get . . . all kinds of things you don't like. And mostly I shut up about it because . . . Well, because I have to. Because you don't want to hear it. But in a thing like this, I have to say something. I just don't like your messing around with this. You hear what I'm saying? I wish . . . I wish I could protect you. Do all kinds of things for you. You won't let me. Okay. I can live with that. People can live with a lot of things. But I can't just keep quiet when you're about to do something foolish. Can I?"

I didn't say anything. I was thinking.

"You angry?"

"No, I'm not angry."

"You going to listen to me?"

"I'll think about it."

"Please!"

"I said I'll think about it."

"Okay."

He got up, sat on the edge of the bed for a moment, and then stood. "I feel like a fool," he said. "I'd better go. I'm sorry."

There was nothing to say to him. I thought of telling him not to go. But if I did that, I felt that I'd have to promise him . . . Well, more than I was ready to promise. Like not going to see Dr. James Harney, for one thing. And not going to Atlanta, for another. I thought about it. Part of me wanted to say the words. I could feel them forming themselves in my head. But it would be worse to say them and not to mean them. Not to live with them. So I said nothing. I sat up, watched him put on his trousers and then his shirt, and then sit down—not on the bed but on a chair—to put on his shoes and socks.

He was waiting for me to say something. I felt that. And that made it more important, somehow, not to say anything that wasn't true. So I just watched him. He put on his tie. And then he gave up waiting. "I'll call you," he said. His voice was controlled but a little husky.

"Do," I said.

He came back to the bed, to my side this time, and he took my face in his hands. He held my face for a moment, and then his hands dropped away. He left.

On the radio, a contralto was still singing the Mahler songs, still languid, still liquid, but much sadder now. I lay there and listened. I must have fallen asleep, because suddenly there was the hiss a radio makes after the station has signed off. I turned it off, tried to get back to sleep and couldn't.

In another time, I thought, or now if I were another kind of person, I could imagine giving in to Martin, to his love and its claims. In a way, it was a lovely prospect. But it can be a drug, and it deadens. One must live one's life. One must live one's own life. Or at least I knew that I must. And in such wispy ways, for such deep, puzzling reasons, I came to my decision.

In the morning I called an old friend. Let her be Mary Jones. The name, in fact, was very nearly as plain as that, which was one reason I had called her. That, and the fact that I could trust her, could rely on her, could impose upon her without explaining too much. What I wanted from her was to borrow, for a little while, her identity. There was no other way to do it, no other safe way. One could not simply approach Harney cold, come in from off the street and complain of depression, fatigue, anxiety, despair, and request a regimen of "vitamins." These people were cagier than that, sailing as they did in shoaled waters. He had, no doubt, learned some of the darker truths of the healing arts from his colleagues, the dispensers of morphia, the performers of abortions back in the old days when the operation was illegal, from the givers of testimony in court cases where the injuries are questionable. These men may be despicable, may be unattractive, but they are not, for the most part, stupid. Stupid doctors—relatively stupid, and there are some, alas—go out into practice and bungle around in well-meaning ways. The world is not so simple and straightforward as we might like to have it.

Well then, to go to Harney, I would have needed to be recommended by someone. Certainly not Charles Elfinstone. A quick telephone call, and that cover would be—I believe the word is *blown*. Nor Lila Swett. But to whom else could I turn? I had wrestled with that question for some time, and then, in a shortcut of wonderful simplicity, I had figured out that I could be recommended at second hand. Such things do happen, and most of us welcome their happening. And let the information have come to me through some improbably prominent figure, to whom Dr. Harney would not think of applying for verification, and I could be rather secure. Ozawa? Bok? White? Someone like that. And my prominent figure would have been talking at a party about some friend who had been helped by Dr. Harney. The friend's name? But of course I would have blanked on that.

For verisimilitude, there ought even to be a touch of skepticism in the remarks of the prominent figure. For verisimilitude and for prudence, too, in order to discourage Harney from checking back.

A frontal attack was no good. The question was what his involvement had been with the burglary in my office, and whether his description of the death of Adam Swett had been accurate and true. Assume that there was anything to hide, in either answer, and no frontal approach could succeed. Assume there was nothing to hide? I could not be losing very much by my assumption of another identity. So I became Mary Jones, labor relations consultant and negotiator. And picked Elliot Richardson as my prominent figure. With an identity, a reference, and a set of symptoms out of Adam Swett's old file, I was prepared, had been prepared for some days now, had been, in fact, so well prepared that I knew, sooner or later, I would be picking up the phone and making the telephone call to request the appointment. I had gone over it so many times in my head, that I seemed to be merely reenacting, to be remembering a very old moment, as I dialed the number, waited for the rings, listened to the receptionist announce the name of her employer.

I had to remember not to blurt out in one incredible rush the story

I had fabricated. I had to make her inquire, answer piecemeal as a real patient, really recommended in this way, might have done. The receptionist, a wary, competent woman, was not quite satisfied, but there was nothing definite enough for her to object to, nothing glaringly improbable enough to put her decidedly and ultimately off. She offered me an appointment with the doctor for the following afternoon. I suppose I should have niggled about the time, complained that there were other appointments that conflicted, ask for alternative times the way patients sometimes do. I thought of it. But I wasn't quite sure enough of myself and my manner, was afraid I might mess it up. And I did have what I had called to get. So I accepted the appointment. Three-thirty the following day. It meant that I had to cancel two patients. But after the true and grand folly of calling Harney's office in the first place, the matter of canceling two patients seemed almost natural.

I told Stanley. I hesitated, but I told him. And he told me I was crazy. "But in a likable way. There are crazies, and there are crazies, right?"

"I suppose I am. But I can't just let it go. And I can't think where else to turn, what else to try. If there is anything to all this, then Dr. Harney is at the middle of it, or very close to the middle. If there isn't anything, then . . ."

"Sure, sure."

"He shouldn't have died of a heart attack. Not at that age, and not in that condition. I mean, it's possible, but it's unlikely. Statistically unlikely."

"You want the body exhumed?"

"It's a thought, isn't it? But not easy to arrange," I said, and then, even as I said it, I thought of Senator Farnsworth.

"If there is a body," Stanley said. "He could have been cremated."

"There was someone else, I think," I said, after a pause. "I should think there might have been a girl. But I don't know for sure. And I wouldn't have the vaguest idea how to start looking for her."

"And if you found her, what could she tell you?"

"I don't know. But then, I don't know what I expect to find out from Harney, and I'm going to see him. Because I have to. Because it would feel worse not to."

"I know what you mean," Stanley said. "What about the police? Have you thought of going to them yet?"

"With what?"

There was no answer. He just shook his head. And picked up a pile of papers to file.

The following afternoon I announced myself as Mary Jones to the receptionist, and gave all the information she asked for. I had absorbed it, and now as her questions squeezed it back out, I felt rather lighter. My address, my phone number, my employment, my office phone number, my health insurance . . . It didn't matter much, this being an office visit; I could give a Blue-Cross/Blue-Shield number. I made one up with the right number of digits. My physician? I thought for a moment, and said I didn't have one. The last doctor I'd seen in Boston, then? That was easy—Martin! I gave his name. The doctor, I was told, by a young woman who looked as if she had been cast for the part from *Marcus Welby* or *General Hospital* —too starchy and too bosomy and with a corolla of platinum-blond hair—would be with me in a moment. I could wait in the lounge. Lounge? Nothing less!

It was one of those buildings on Bay State Road, once a residence, now a series of doctors' offices. Harney seemed to be doing well, whatever it was he was doing. He had a very large suite on the ground floor, with a waiting room—or lounge—all full of Knoll and Henry Miller, with a bronze Directional sideboard for magazines. It screamed money, or no, whispered commandingly, for it was in splendid taste, the best taste money could buy. A little cold, perhaps? Or was I being mean and unfair. I didn't, after all, like the man.

Perhaps that was a mistake. One ought to be as blank as possible, as open as possible, in order to pick up clearly and without distortion. The receptionist came into the room to let me know that Dr. Harney would see me, and she led me back to his office. He came around his desk to offer me a chair, then returned to his chair and looked at the card the receptionist had given him.

"Yes," he said, looking up at me. "Now what seems to be the problem?"

His diction was pleasantly precise, matching in many ways his person. He had steel-gray hair, impressively barbered. He wore an elegantly casual suit, a very light gray flannel of extremely conservative cut, so that the effect was both correct and yet relaxed. And the grays of suit and hair were not unrelated. The face was rather long, interestingly bony, and punctuated with jet-black eyebrows that were all the more noticeable because of the color of his hair. Dyed? Not likely, but it was possible. It would have been a brilliant touch had it been deliberately calculated. Brown eyes. The mouth, in repose, was melancholy. No flashed politician's smile that a lot of doctors use as bedside—or office—manner.

I explained to him that I had been tired lately, had been a little depressed, that I was losing interest in my work, and that I had thought about going to a psychiatrist about it, but that just didn't feel right. I wasn't sure I trusted psychiatrists—or psychiatry, really.

"I understand," he said. "But then, how do you trust me? How do you trust any doctor?"

"You don't really. Or I don't," I said. "But I heard about you . . . that you do things with vitamins. That seemed less menacing somehow."

"You know one of my patients?"

I did the bit about hearing from Elliot Richardson about someone he knew who had been a patient. That it was vitamins. That the man had just turned around in a matter of weeks, seemed younger, more vital, more energetic. "It seemed to fit," I said. "At least, it was close enough so that I thought I ought to come and talk to you. To find out if it really fits, this vitamin thing and my own . . . I don't know. *Condition* is too strong for it. I don't think I'm really sick. It's something between sickness and health."

"That's where most people are," Dr. Harney said, looking up at the ceiling. Relaxing? Or thinking? "Somewhere between sickness and health."

"That's why it's hard to know how to say it. I feel a little bit silly even being here, taking up your time . . ."

"No, no. Not at all. Medicine ought to be concerned with degrees of health, don't you think? Sickness, of course, but degrees of health. What is it that you do?"

I laid out Mary Jones's life for him. It was not exactly what I could have made up, but it was close enough to what I had extrapolated from Elfinstone and from Swett at least to qualify. And it was entirely possible, even likely, that Dr. Harney would check on what I was telling him. So I spoke the truth. Somebody else's truth, but the truth.

"I see," he said, with some sympathy, some warmth even. "I see it, I have seen it. You're quite right. You're not sick. You are suffering what many of us suffer . . ."

There was a long pause. I was being invited to ask what that was. I asked.

"The twentieth century. The kinds of stress that have been placed on us, the demands of our civilization, of our society . . . The effect is physical, emotional, mental. It would have to be, wouldn't it?"

"I imagine so," I said. "But is there anything that can be done for it?"

"In the long run, no. Not unless we change our entire society. Or drop out of the society around us. Those people who go up to Vermont and build log cabins with their hands . . . They are treating themselves. And they may be doing the right thing. But that doesn't quite fit into your life, does it?"

"Not exactly," I said. I suppose it was about at this point that I felt myself relaxing a little. I could see where he was going, could imagine the rest of the argument, but I could not fault it. I could disagree with it, but even as Mary Jones, or as Adam Swett or Charles Elfinstone, I could have disagreed with it. There was no pressure, no coercion. He was not, perhaps, such a bad man. He was more plausible than I had expected. But how much more?

"There are other things to do. These vitamins . . . And there are shots, and there is more to them than just vitamins. Hormones as well. Other substances . . . It all depends on your physical condition and on the stresses of your life, of your . . . condition, I think was your word."

"Yes," I said.

"It's a bargain. You can make it if you want to, or decide that you don't want to or shouldn't. It's entirely up to you. You can imagine it as . . . well, as an automobile. You can drive at forty miles an hour, and go a very long time, with better gas mileage and less wear and tear on the machine. Or you can push your foot down a little on the accelerator and go seventy miles an hour. You run out of gas faster, and it's harder on the engine. Those are ethical choices, philosophical choices. I don't make them. You make them for yourself. You understand?"

"I think so."

"No questions?"

"Well, one. Can I undertake this . . . this course of treatment for a while? And then stop? I mean, just to get me out of where I am, past it."

"You can. It isn't always easy. There is a kind of exhilaration, after all, a sense of power . . . More than a sense, because you operate with more power. It takes a very firm decision to decide to abandon that. Again, that's another ethical choice, isn't it? But yes, it's possible. And it happens. It is sometimes difficult, and that's something you should think about."

"If I did decide to go ahead, when would it begin? What would you do?"

"Now? Nothing. Now you are to go and think. Take a few days. A week. Think hard about yourself and your life and what you want. And then, if you like, come back. We'll do a physical, and check you out that way. And then I'll think. And if we both decide that this is what's good for you, and that we ought to go ahead, we can do that. Fair enough?"

"More than fair," I said.

"It's not an easy decision to make," he said, after a perhaps intentionally dramatic pause. "What it requires is that you take a hard look at yourself, at your life, at what you want. At what you're willing to settle for. One of my patients told me that he'd found a line in Plutarch that seemed to bear on his decision. I don't urge this, but I pass it on. What Plutarch said was that the scale of life is beautiful, not its length of time. It comes down to something like that. You follow me?"

He looked at me, a hard, clear gaze, inquiring, challenging, even, perhaps, warning.

I sensed that it was part of his performance, was the way he generally concluded these initial interviews. And I got up to leave. I had to admit that he had been perfectly fair about it. No misleading promises. On the contrary, he had been carefully balanced. He had not used the dread word, had not actually said *amphetamines*. But to a layman, the word would not carry any more than his carefully balanced promises and cautions. Perhaps less. It was not, after all, beyond the limits of medical ethics to describe the effect of a medication without actually naming it. I could not fault him.

I promised to think carefully, and to let him know as soon as I had made up my mind.

"Sometimes," he said, "it can be helpful simply to know that there can be help. You may feel better just from having had this talk. It has happened. And I'm pleased when it does. Pay attention to that, too, to how you feel. Take your time."

I thanked him. I promised once more that I would let him know. I went out through the receptionist's office and out to the street. I suppose I was disappointed. I had expected . . . what? A monster? A mad Dr. Frankenstein? A movie villain? No, nothing quite so extreme, but I had counted on having certain unfavorable reactions, to feeling suspicion, to experiencing some antipathy. I found, instead, that I rather liked the man.

Eleven

Okay, so he was a wonderful fellow. A fine doctor, an admirable human being. All those things. There were still a few loose ends that I could tug at, a few questions that were outstanding, waiting for me to worry at them. If I had the inclination to do that, the energy, the certainty, I could pursue them. But did I? Did it matter?

Figure the worst, that he was sitting there in that opulent office, junking his patients up to the eyeballs, letting them fly on amphetamines or whatever combination of goodies he brewed up in the basement, there was nothing to object to in the way he did it. He came on straight enough, and presented the choice honestly enough. I had to agree with him that it wasn't simply a medical question, but a philosophical question. Plutarch? But I remembered what Dr. Herndon had told me about Adam Swett and how Swett had talked a lot about Nietzsche. The second philosophical dose? The stronger intellectual medicine to which Harney turned when the effectiveness of the Plutarch had worn off?

Even assuming that there was some such progression, how was I to judge philosophical positions? Outside my competence. Medical training, even psychiatric training, is not a preparation for that kind of evaluation. It was perfectly possible that these ideas might have some validity, and that their implications for medical practice might produce . . . well, some such approach as Harney seemed to have been making. Let the patient decide, and serve as his willing accomplice? No, he exercised some control, refused patients—or said he did—who were not qualified, physically, to mess around with these "substances." And he controlled, presumably, the dosage of the pa-

82

tients according to their needs, their tolerances. What was wrong with it?

In that mood, I could even imagine some scenario in which Swett somehow contributed to his own death, exceeded the prescribed dosage, ignored the doctor's instructions, tried even to pressure Harney into taking him back again . . . Something of that kind. But the heart attack? And then, behind it all, so far back as now to seem almost insignificant, the one sure fact of my house having been burglarized, my files having been invaded. Elfinstone's book. Why hadn't Harney merely called me to ask whatever it was he wanted to know? Or had Elfinstone not been acting for Harney at all? Had it been some independent enterprise?

Obviously, the thing to do was to call Mrs. Swett and ask her if she had ever heard of Elfinstone. I had perhaps jumped ahead of myself, making conclusions that were incorrect and then trying to build on them. I had gone from Elfinstone to Harney because he was a connection between Elfinstone and Swett. But the only connection? A coincidence, perhaps? Mrs. Swett could tell me, if she would. Or if she dared. There had been fear in that woman, anger and fear. And I was reluctant to impose. At least until I absolutely had to.

It was remembering her manner, the tension that she had shown me—occasioned by my inquiries about Dr. Harney—that I began to turn back to my original notion. My hunch could not have been so far off. It was only that there was such openness, such reassurance in Dr. James Harney . . .

But was I to be taken in by that? Did I believe it? Did I want to believe it?

I called Martin and told him I wanted to see him.

"Dinner?" he offered.

"Sure, fine."

"I can watch you eat more eggplant, eh?"

"Don't be hostile. I don't need it. Not today."

"Sorry. And it wasn't very hostile. A joke."

"Jokes can be hostile," I reminded him. "I'm just a little edgy. I'm sorry."

"No need to be sorry. If you can't be edgy with me, then with whom? No, no, don't answer that. Anyway, I'll see you this evening. Seven?"

"Fine. And thanks."

"Thank you! I like it when you call me. You know that, don't you?"

"Yes, I know."

Confusing? Complicated? But what isn't? I found myself resenting his proprietary air, but at the same time I was awfully glad to have him to call, to have his concern to rely on. One can't have it both ways, and yet, unresolved, both feelings were there, not in conflict really, but just there, not touching, like lines on two different planes. Is that a metaphor, or is there some kind of geometry of the psyche, some spatial analogue . . . a professional's defense, of course. Seize one's own feelings and turn them into an exhibit for the clinician, then become the clinician and duck the whole thing, as I suspect Freud did, himself. An interesting notion. I would have to bring it up, sometime, with Dr. Brinton. Dr. Clare Brinton was the woman with whom I did my didactic analysis, a grande dame who trained in London with the fugitive Viennese, and, most important, a friend. It was good even to think about her . . .

But I had to think about other people, other problems. I had re-scheduled two patients in order to go and see Dr. Harney. There were two more who would be picking the plants in my waiting room to pieces. Plastic plants are no good. They last, but they are not satis-fying to pick at. So I buy cheap real ones at the five and ten, sacri-fices to neurosis. A hardy plant will last maybe a week. But never mind the plants. I am, I tell myself, helping people. It is a judgment one makes, preferring people to plants, a more conservative judg-ment, no doubt, than those Dr. Harney made, or allowed his patients to make, but a judgment no less.

I drank a glass of ice water, and turned my attention to my prac-tice, and to such questions as whether a twelve-year-old who thinks he's invisible is merely fanciful or possibly sick . . .

That evening Martin came by, and after we had drinks we went out to our usual place in the North End. He was as good as I knew he would be, didn't push, didn't ask any questions, was just there, and happy to be there. Which made it easier to talk to him, which I did over spumoni and coffee.

"I went to see Harney," I said.

"You did?"

I nodded.

"And he said he didn't kill anybody and didn't break into your office, right?"

"I didn't ask him that."

"You just let him free-associate? And nothing came up about murder or burglary?"

"I pretended to be a patient. I told him I was Mary Jones. I told him I was tired and a little depressed, and that I'd heard about him from Elliot Richardson . . ."

"You what? You know you're out of your mind?"

"I don't think so."

"Well, I do. You may be the psychiatrist, but I'm a goddamn doctor too. And I think you're crazy."

"Well, if you get a call from him . . ."

"Me?"

"He wanted to know who my doctor was. Mary Jones's doctor. I gave him your name."

"Thanks a lot. That's just swell."

"Tell him I'm healthy."

"What for? You're not planning to go back there, are you?"

"I don't know. I think he's pushing amphetamines . . ."

"So? What do you care? Lots of guys do that."

"But . . ." But then I stopped. I just didn't know any more. I told him about Harney and what he had been like, how honest he'd been about the way he'd laid out the decision for me to make, how straight he'd been with me. And we talked for a while about the questions—Harney's philosophical questions—that arose from the making of that decision.

"I don't know. He doesn't sound so bad to me. There are lots worse around, I'll tell you."

"I know that."

"So? Leave him alone. Forget it."

"What about Swett? What about my files?"

"To hell with them."

"That's easy to say," I said.

"Then for God's sake, say it! Look, I can't tell you what to do. I'm not telling you. I'm . . . I'm advising, the way I'd advise any friend. Don't get your damned back up about it. Listen to me, the way you'd listen to any friend. Would you do that? It just doesn't make any sense. It isn't reasonable what you're doing. Running around, asking questions, making trips down to New Haven, pretending to be Mary Jones . . . It's crazy!"

I was angry and not angry. I knew that his intentions were friendly, were loving. And I even wondered whether he might not be right. Was I blowing this thing up out of all proportion? And then, because I had thought of her earlier in the day, I thought again of Dr. Brinton, of Clare . . .

"It's possible," I said. "I can't be sure."

"I'm telling you—" he started to say.

"No, no. I haven't finished. I had a thought. I wonder whether I ought to talk to my analyst about it. You think?"

"You trust her?"

"Of course I trust her."

"Then talk to her. She'll tell you exactly what I'm telling you right now."

"That I'm crazy?"

"No, not that you're crazy. That it's crazy. That you should cut it the hell out. That you're a psychiatrist and not a detective. That you should go to the police if you want to, and then just forget about it. Walk away from it. That's what she'll tell you. I'm sure of it."

"All right, I will."

"Call her. Call her tonight. Or tomorrow morning."

"I may go to New York to see her."

"If that's what you want to do, then go to New York."

"And if she thinks I'm right?"

"Then you're both crazy."

"But you'll tell Harney that Mary Jones is physically healthy and all that?"

"If Dr. Brinton thinks that this is a good idea, this thing, I'll tell Harney anything you like."

"Promise?"

"Wait a minute! You're going to let him shoot you up with junk?"

"If I have to."

"Tell your analyst that, will you? Just tell her. You promise me that, and I'll promise you anything you please."

"A deal," I said. And we drank to it with the fresh coffee that the waiter brought.

"You know," Martin said, "now that we've got our deal, I'll tell you what I've been thinking about. I don't even know whether it's relevant. But it's been going through my mind, or just sitting there during the last ten minutes, an image, something I saw yesterday. I was coming out of the hospital, and in a hurry. We're always in a hurry, aren't we? Anyway, there was a guy, a bum, really, lying

86

on the sidewalk. I guess he was sleeping. He might have been sleeping. But it was cool, and I wouldn't want to be sleeping on the sidewalk in that kind of weather. Hell, I wouldn't sleep on the sidewalk at all. This isn't Calcutta, for God's sake, it's Boston! And this was in front of a hospital, right? Maybe sixty, maybe a hundred doctors an hour were walking right by this guy. And maybe three hundred nurses. Cops, the emergency-room squad, the whole crew. You think anybody stopped? Nobody stopped. Nobody took the time or the risk. He could have been in heart failure, could have been in coma, anything . . . We're supposed to be a helping profession? God help us."

"So you do see what I mean?"

"I do and I don't. I mean, there are other people who need it more. You're not going to be able to do much, are you? Even if you went ahead and found out who broke into your office, and what for, and how Swett died . . . There are all kinds of people around, desperate for help, and we just walk by them. Because we have to. Because we'd go crazy if we didn't. Because . . . I don't know. Because maybe the guy has a right to sleep on the sidewalk if he wants to, to be left alone. If he wanted to ask for help, he could have. If he was conscious, anyway. I guess what got me is that it was right in front of the hospital! Two blocks away, I might not have noticed it, or not quite that same way."

"Why didn't you stop?"

"I was late for an appointment with a guy from Washington. To talk about health care delivery and emergency service. To talk about how to help guys lying on the sidewalk. I guess that's what gets me. I mean, it could be eight hundred thousand dollars we can get. But to help that bum . . ."

"At least you worry about it still."

"And I understand your worry. But . . . Oh, hell! I still think you ought to let it go. You can make up for it by stopping next time you see a bum on the sidewalk. If you don't mind the risk of getting sued . . . which is why we tell ourselves that we ought to walk on by, but I wonder."

We walked for a little after dinner, and then Martin took me home. I asked him if he would mind very much if I didn't ask him in for a nightcap. I wanted to think. He was very good, said he understood, and maybe he did. He kissed me gently on the cheek. Then he ran the ball of his index finger along the line of my jaw.

"Go on," he said. "Go think." His voice was full of tender concern. I promised myself that after I'd worked out this present mess, I would think about him, about us.

In the morning I called Clare Brinton and told her I needed to see her.

"Yes, of course," she said. "When?"

She was, of course, leaving it to me to decide and demonstrate how urgent the need was. A couple of hours? This evening? Saturday?

"Would this evening be all right? I could fly down after my last patient . . ."

"Yes, of course," she said. "Dinner?"

It was a gracious invitation, but also another kind of inquiry. How clinical, how professional was the visit? How formal did I want the meeting to be?

"Dinner would be fine," I told her.

"Good," she said, expressing perhaps some relief that the trouble was not entirely crippling for me. "Come right from the airport. I shall be here."

"Thank you," I said.

Very crisply, she replied, "Not at all," this being, after all, her vocation, her life.

In her seventies now, she sees very few patients. She has one or two analysands in training, confers sometimes on evaluations of other doctors' puzzling patients, still writes a good deal, but she has restricted herself, adjusting her work to her physical capacities, as a lot of less sensible doctors never manage to do. I was, I knew, imposing on her, but it would have been insulting and diminishing not to impose, not to call on her. It would have been a declaration— or a confession—that I thought her usefulness was ended. All that, somehow, was in her retort. And it was bracing, felt good to have been reminded that way. It was like old times.

Twelve

On the plane to New York, I thought about . . .

Good Lord! That certainly does sound like the kind of start a patient is likely to make. A way into whatever is really bothering her that seems conversational, casual. I thought about what to tell Clare, how to explain it to her. Yes, but also I thought about Clare, about how it had been with her, how she had led me into myself. Imposing herself upon me? Offering herself for me to struggle with? Doing all the delicate, terrible things that need to be done in order to help another person find herself. And this was what I presumed to do with my patients, feeling sometimes that I was competent and helpful, and yet other times feeling that I was an impostor, that it was Clare they really should be seeing, my mentor, my analyst, my mother-figure . . . All that.

And to avoid brooding about it too much—I was going to be seeing Clare for an evening, not for a month—I seized on small things, distractions. As, for instance, how hopeful it was that I should be flying to see her, the whole stupid thing having begun, really, at an airport, in that bookstand. Not that either airport had any real significance, but we accept these totems and symbols, and cling to them in the hope of finding some sense and order to our lives. I also thought about all the doctors I had been talking to—Herndon, and Harney, and Martin of course, and now Clare. And about Martin's sidewalk bum and the affront he posed to the entire profession. More serious, perhaps, than Harney's affront, if Harney was an affront. Harney might be wrong, but there was room for error in the world. Indifference is more likely to do us in.

The question, though, was whether I might not be masking another kind of indifference myself, whether I had not become obsessive about this business of the burglary and Harney and Swett. And that was how to begin.

I got to Clare's apartment a little after seven. I recognized things from the old apartment, the one she'd had on the West Side when I had been in training and had gone to see her every day. The big Sheraton breakfront, the Chinese silk screen on the ebony-and-ivory frame. They were the same and not the same. Less comfortable here in the East Side box she lived in now. I had seen the apartment before, had been in it a number of times, but I still think of that great flat on Central Park West with the columns at the entrance to the living room and the arches over the windows . . .

Clare looked . . . not well. She was even thinner than she had been last time I'd seen her, and there was something about the eyes that was different. She had become an ageless kind of bright-eyed bird, had seemed to be set somewhere about sixty in a way that would last forever; but the eyes were less bright now and the gestures less sharp. The way she cocked her head a little to one side—which had always seemed to indicate a quality of attention, skeptical, amused, and very sharp—now seemed to be a way of straining just to hear.

She offered me a sherry, and I accepted. She had a very small sherry, herself. And then we went downstairs to the restaurant in the building. "For you," she said, "they have onion soup and a good quiche."

Over dinner and a half-bottle of white wine, I told her about what had happened, how it had started, where my investigation had led, what my intuitions were, all of it. She listened, head at that slight slant except when she was actually eating. From time to time she asked a question. She didn't say very much. I felt rather disappointed.

We drank our coffee almost in silence. Was she not interested? Had I made a mistake in coming down to see her? I resented the cost of the flight. No, no, I didn't. I resented the way in which I had been depending on her, had assumed that big mamma could just listen to my recitation and then wave her hand and make all the problems go away. Well, if that was true, then I had learned something worth the airfare and the dinner tab.

But she said, "Come, we'll go back upstairs now. We'll talk there." And we went back to the apartment, where she asked more questions, more probing questions, obvious questions that I had some-how neglected to ask myself.

"Who was hurt?"

"I don't know. Perhaps Swett. I'm not sure."

"What about you?"

"I wasn't hurt much. I didn't even know about the break-in until I read the paperback . . ."

"But then you were hurt?"

"I don't know that I was hurt. Angry . . ."

"Violated?"

She gave me a look of exasperation, as one might give a slow student. Which, of course, was what I was. "Your house? Your room? Your files? Boxes, I should think?"

Well, all right. It was a classic connection, and I was able to make it. In fact, I had made it. I remembered thinking on the plane that it had been a kind of rape, but I'd blocked it out. And now Dr. Brinton brought it back for me. If my person had been violated by the burglary, I was certainly going to react. But was that all I had been doing?

"What about men?" she asked.

I told her about John, and about Martin.

"Martin is the more important one?"

Yes, he was. I said so.

"But you mentioned John first. For distance? To protect yourself? You are afraid still? Or cautious?"

"Probably."

"Which brings you back to the feeling of violation, perhaps?"

"Yes, it's possible. It makes a pattern. But is that all? Is that the only reason?"

"Martin said that you were crazy. Such talk from a doctor! Still, there is something unusual here. You recognize it yourself. You called me, after all . . ."

"Yes, yes I did. But for practical advice as much as for anal-ysis . . ."

"How can there be practical advice without analysis? How can we solve problems when we don't understand the nature of the problems? Is this a science or is it witchcraft? You must begin to make these decisions for yourself, to take positions."

"I know what you mean. And I agree with you . . ."

"No, don't agree with me. Independently think out what you are doing, what it means, what it is."

"Yes."

"Do you think Swett was murdered?"

"I don't know. I wonder about it."

"If he was murdered, do you think Dr. Harney had anything to do with it? Or Mr. Elfinstone?"

"It's possible. I can't really tell."

"Then wait. Have patience. Let it go, and try to relax and to be passive. There are active roles and passive roles, and one must learn to distinguish which ones are appropriate."

"But that theory of yours is for analysis, not for criminology."

"What's the difference? It is for living! It is biological, and psychological, and experiential. When to hold tight and when to let go! When to push and when not to push. Ecclesiastes! It is for all living."

"Let it go, then?"

"For a while. And if nothing forces you to come back to it, then you can let it go for good. We don't always have cures, but remissions are welcome, are they not?"

"Yes, I suppose they are."

"Of course they are. And get locks for your files." There was, with that, a small smile, amused, affectionate. I delighted in it, not only for myself, but for Clare, too. She had seemed . . . well, not abstract, and not at all vague. She was quite brilliant. But a little as though she were functioning out of habit, inertia.

"Is there anything else on your mind?" she asked.

"No. Nothing worth talking about."

"Good. Then you will have a brandy, and I shall watch you, and we can talk worthlessly."

She waved her hand toward the bar cart. I got the brandy. Would she have anything? A glass of Perrier and ice. I brought it to her. We sat in the living room like two old friends now, which we were.

"Your work goes well?"

"Oh, yes. It's fine. Interesting. Keeps me busy, but I like that."

"Yes, it can be busy."

"And you? How are things with you?"

"Not good. The body wears out. I am ill."

"I'm sorry."

"Yes," she said, and sighed. "I know, I know. I am an old woman. It happens. Sickness and death."

I tried to think of what to say. It would have been difficult enough with anyone else, but to her? I had already said I was sorry. To repeat it would be useless. I nodded. I reached out and touched her hand, delicate as a bird's foot. And soon the bird would fly away.

I raised my brandy glass, held it for a moment, and then sipped. "I don't know how to thank you," I said. "Not just for today. For everything."

"Be as good as I am," she said. "If you can, be better." It was a kind of challenge. It was a valediction. I drained the glass.

"You have a plane to catch," she said, "and I am tired." I was dismissed.

On the way back to Boston, I didn't think about anything else. Only about her, what a fine woman she was. And felt anger. We get used to death. We see a lot of it, at any rate, and we develop a carapace, need to in order to survive. Toughened by internship and residence, toughened by the stupid repetitions of death, we learn . . . to walk over men in the gutter? Perhaps. But Clare Brinton had not so toughened herself as to lose touch, lose sympathy. Nor had Martin, nor John. Nor, I hoped, had I. It is never easy. The body changes. You can see it, alive at one moment and then not alive, and the color is different. Something has gone out of it. The Greeks thought of the spirit as butterflies and represented their dead with butterflies coming up out of their mouths and flying away. Not far wrong.

The plane landed at Logan a little after one in the morning. I found my car and drove home. And then lay awake for a while, feeling alone and bereft. It was nearly three before I fell asleep.

The next day was just torture. I was exhausted, and it was like a nightmare in which you are running through tapioca. The toaster broke. There was a traffic tie-up on Storrow Drive. The clinic was a madhouse, and I had to attend a meeting of thrilling pointlessness. Of course it dragged on forever, and I had no chance for lunch. With only ten minutes to spare, I got back to the house to see my private patients.

Stanley was waiting for me. He seemed very cheerful. I told him I was late, and busy, and exhausted, and hungry, cutting him off from any garrulity.

"I've found Swett's girl," he announced. "I mean, I haven't actually found her, but I know her name. She's an instructor at B.U. Heard about her last night. I thought you'd be pleased."

"I am, Stanley, I am. But I'm . . . Well, I'm not so sure I want to go on with this any more."

"Okay," he said. "You da boss!"

"Oh, cut it out."

"Here's her name," he said. He handed me a three-by-five card on which he had written the name. Helene Purvis. I noted, with some distaste, the final *e* of the first name.

I thanked Stanley, looked at the card again, and stuck it in the drawer. To hell with it. I had promised Martin that I'd do what Clare Brinton told me to do. I had promised Clare . . .

Well, no, I hadn't actually promised her anything specific, had I? But I felt the obligation. To be as good as she is. At least to try.

And there were patients waiting to see me, occasions for that trying. More important things to do with my time.

Forget about it?

Yes.

Part Two

One

It was not a disappearance, but a transformation. The questions Dr. Brinton had raised, the connections she had suggested, continued to occupy my thoughts. I was no longer concerned with the crime—if there was a crime—but with my reaction. It is not required of psychiatrists that they be healthier than their patients. If it were, there would be very few who were qualified to practice. But it is necessary that psychiatrists have some understanding of their own psyches, their own biases, their own idiosyncrasies in order to be able to adjust, to compensate, and to present to their patients something approaching an objective view.

I was disturbed then, not because of the burglary but because I had neglected my own continuing self-examination, my own continuing struggle for understanding and balance. One can take for granted so many things about one's life, can come to believe that one is *finished*. We can be seduced into such a frame of mind by the temporary equilibrium we have arranged, by the sheer luck of not having been challenged or disturbed for months at a time. The world seems more and more reasonable; the need for change or even for alertness drops off . . .

I reviewed my work with my patients, looking at each of my cases with as fresh an eye as I could bring to the work. Less certain of myself, less confident of my own adjustments, I was able to be more open, more receptive to some of the things my patients had been trying to communicate. I was able to make connections—and to help them make connections—that had been previously elusive and obscure. Great progress, great excitement, and at the same time, a great diffidence on my part combined to make for a very exciting six weeks. I made progress with my patients, and with myself as well, remembering ways in which I had envied the boys in the sixth grade when my class did a project on the Middle Ages and there were pictures of armor all around the classroom. I envied them because only males wore armor, and this seemed to me unfair. Because boys don't need armor, do not have to face the prospect of having their bodies penetrated, invaded . . . And at a time just before puberty, I was concerned, must have been concerned, about the biological prospects I was facing.

Not in itself all that exciting, or even interesting. But as a way of remembering what that time had been like, how I had grown and been formed in that period of development, it was useful as a connection with other insights that had come out of my analysis, and out of my life as an analyst. A creative period, uncomfortable, as many creative periods can be, but also exciting. If the occasion had been a foolish burglary a long time before, that hardly seemed to matter.

But then one morning I read a report in the Boston *Globe*. Edward J. Curran, forty-two, a member of the Boston Finance Committee and attorney in private practice, had jumped to his death from the top of the Hancock Building. There was a sizable article about it, the spectacular nature of the suicide combining with Curran's prominence in Boston politics to warrant a lot of space. I read the piece, feeling exactly the queasiness and sadness that the reporter must have felt. It was a peculiar death. Curran had prepared a packet with his will, his insurance policies, his securities . . . Very rational and businesslike, and odd for a man named Curran. A Catholic? Well, even for a lapsed Catholic, there is at least a prejudice about suicide, a taboo which may not keep a sufficiently distraught person from taking his life, but which makes it improbable that he will do it in so calculated and so orderly a way.

And then, down in the body of the story, after the tributes and expressions of shock from his friends and associates, there was the one line: "Mr. Curran's physician, Dr. James Harney, had no comment."

I could just bet he didn't. It took me a minute to think why the reporter would have called the doctor, or why the police would have called him. But then, it seemed reasonable enough. Allow Curran some fatal illness, some degenerative disease, and there would be a reason . . . Enough reason for a Catholic? Perhaps. But no comment meant no disease, no long, painful, expensive death he had leapt to anticipate. Forty-two! A young man, active, promising, and . . . the perfect Harney patient.

I thought first of calling the *Globe,* of speaking to the reporter to try to find out more. Had there been, in all that orderly compilation of papers, a note? But no, I couldn't ask questions of any reporter without explaining who I was, what my interest was, what I knew. Did I want to do that? If it became necessary, if there were no other way, I might. But there was at least one other way, more discreet, more appealing. I called Senator Farnsworth. He was not yet in his office. I drove down to the clinic and called him again. This time I got him.

"Sarah! What can I do for you?"

"I want to find out more about Edward Curran," I said.

"A terrible thing. Very sad. What do you want to know?"

"Whether there was a note. What the note said. Why he killed himself . . ."

"I thought you might call," Senator Farnsworth said. "I've been wondering what you've been up to."

"Nothing, really. I'd dropped it, that thing we were talking about. I'd written it off. But now I'm not so sure."

"Is there a connection? Between that and Curran?"

"I don't know. There might be. I want to find out."

"All right, I'll do what I can. I'll get back to you this afternoon."

"Thank you."

"Not at all. I offered, remember?"

"I can still be grateful."

It was not difficult for the senator to find out what I wanted to know. A phone call to a friend in the district attorney's office, or to a captain in the right precinct, and he could get anything he wanted— anything within reasonable limits. I thought of this during the day, not knowing whether or not to hope that he would call back with the text of the note. If there were an investigation, if the police were looking into the death, into all its circumstances, into Dr. James Harney—then I was excused. I could simply go to them and report what I knew. No, what I suspected. And I would be free of it. But if there were an investigation, then Senator Farnsworth might have at least a little difficulty, might find them reluctant to share evidence . . .

But there was no trouble at all. He called me that afternoon, and he had the text of Curran's brief note. He read it to me on the phone, and I wrote it out: *My only regrets are for the pain my death may cause to others. I assure them that this is a rational, considered action, that I am sorry to leave them, but that my reasons are good and sufficient. Modesty and gentleness are worth all of Nietzsche. I made wrong choices and cannot go back. All I can do is obliterate. I ask Franny to forgive me, and know that my last thoughts are not only of her but of the life we should have had, if things had been different.*

"Does that make any sense to you?" the senator asked.

"I'm afraid so," I told him. "Enough sense."

"Is there anything else I can do?"

"I don't know yet. Let me think about it for a while. If this means what I think it does, I'd like to come and talk to you about it. There may be a lot you can do . . ."

"I'm at your service," he said, being courtly but meaning it.

"I know. And thank you."

I hung up and I sat there, back where I had been weeks before. Or worse off now, because I had been wrong to let it go. Perhaps if I had plodded ahead, Curran might not have had to kill himself. Maybe he could have been helped. But the sign was there, as big as a billboard, as bright as neon: Nietzsche . . . Not your standard bedside philosopher for an Irish-Catholic politician and lawyer in Boston.

"Who has been hurt?" Clare had asked. And I had been unable to give a definite answer. Suspicions, hunches, but nothing certain. It was different now. There was not yet anything that I felt I could go to the police with, their rules of evidence being different from those of psychiatry. But for me, the repetition of Nietzsche's name was as definite and certain as the glow in Madame Curie's pots from the radium. I thought of calling Clare to tell her, but didn't. She had enough to think about, enough to deal with. And one of her messages to me had been that I would have to be independent now, would have to learn to stand by myself, analyze myself, direct myself without any more help from her.

I rummaged around in my desk drawers and found the three-by-five card on which Stanley had written the name of Swett's . . . mistress? casual friend? companion? Well, I would find out. I would at least go to see Helene Purvis.

And then? The difficulty was that there might be enough about Adam Swett to interest the authorities, or there might not. There could be some connection—obviously through Dr. Harney—between

Swett and Edward Curran. But the likelihood was that neither death, by itself, would be enough, and that unless the connection could be established, could be legally proved, it would have no effect. Like psychiatry, the administration of justice is forced to operate at some distance from the domains of common sense. But I would worry about those things later.

I asked Stanley about Helene Purvis, how he had heard about her and where to find her. He was, not unreasonably, surprised.

"I thought you'd given all that up," he said.

"I did. I had."

I showed him the Boston *Globe* and pointed to the piece about Curran's suicide. He read it, then handed it back to me without a word.

"Well?" I asked.

"Well, all right. So you're interested again. I can understand that."

There was something of an edge in his voice. I didn't quite understand what it was, or why it should be there. "What's the matter?" I asked.

"Nothing."

"You don't sound as if nothing's the matter."

"What I sound like has nothing to do with it. It's nothing for us to talk about."

"Why not?"

"You don't want to hear it. I don't want to say it. It probably isn't even true, anyway."

"What isn't? For God's sake, Stanley, why are we playing games?"

"We always play games, don't we?"

"All right, let's stop. Let's talk straight for a change. What is it that's bothering you?"

He sat down in the chair where patients sit. Deliberately? It was the nearest chair, but still . . . Or was it the way he seemed to be choosing his words, the way he was working out a presentation that combined with his presence in that particular chair to make me think about patients? At any rate, I behaved as I would have behaved with a patient, waiting, not pushing, letting him take his time.

"It probably isn't fair," he said at last, "but still what it looks like is . . ." He broke off. Then he hunched his shoulders forward and started again. "There's a black guy, see. And he died. And you were looking into it for a while, were all upset about it. You cared. And then you stopped caring. You let it go. I got the name of the girl for you, and you just put it in the drawer there and forgot about it. And now a white guy dies, and it's important. More important because it was a white guy this time? I don't think so. Don't want to think so. But you learn to watch that kind of stuff. There's a lot of it. It could be that that's what you think even if you don't know you think it, you know?"

"It's not true, Stanley. It isn't true."

He looked at me, wanting to believe. I told him about my talk with Dr. Brinton, and how she had advised me to wait, to be more passive, to let the world tell me what to do. To go with the flow. "It would have been just the same if the order had been reversed, if the first man had been white and the second man had been black. Or if both had been white. Or if both had been black."

He nodded.

"It isn't just the coincidence of Harney's having treated both of them. It's Nietzsche."

"It's what?"

I told him about what Dr. Herndon had told me about Swett's talking of Nietzsche. And about Curran's suicide note. "So you see, it isn't color. Color has nothing to do with it."

"Okay," he said. "I was wrong. But better to bring it out and talk about it than to wonder and keep quiet."

"I'm glad you did."

"You want me to come with you when you talk to Helene Purvis?"

"Let me try her alone, first. Then, if that doesn't work, you can try. It's hard to know in a thing like this whether it's better to be a woman or to be black . . ."

"Women's liberation says it feels about the same," he said, the smile back, the wise guy reestablished.

"I meant for getting her confidence, for getting her to talk."

"I know what you mean. I was only offering."

"We'll see. I may need you."

He nodded, stood up, stretched—as patients often do, tired from the effort of sitting there and speaking as precisely as they can about great, vague, menacing things in their lives—and then told me, "She lives in Somerville. She's in the phone book."

"Thanks," I said, not only meaning it to apply to the information about Helene Purvis.

"Right," he said. Meaning that it was all right? That I had been right? That we were right again? Perhaps all those things.

I called Helene Purvis, told her that I wanted to talk to her about Adam Swett, that I had been his doctor for a little while, and that I believed she had known him.

"Yes," she said. "I knew him."

"Could I see you? I shouldn't be bothering you if it weren't important."

She hesitated. Then she agreed.

I asked when would be convenient for her. I told her I'd be glad to come out to her house. She invited me to come that evening. "Eight-thirty, nine, whenever . . ."

I said I'd be there between eight-thirty and nine.

Later on that afternoon Martin called to find out how I was, to share some news with me about progress he was making with his funding efforts for the emergency-room project, and almost by the way to ask me to dinner. "We could make an evening of it," he said suggestively.

"I'm sorry. I'd love to, but I . . . have another engagement."

"Oh?"

I said nothing.

"All right, then," he said. "Perhaps another time."

"Of course another time!"

"You did lay it down there pretty heavily. 'Another engagement!' Some kind of a challenge? Trying to make me jealous?"

"No. It isn't that."

"Okay," he said. "It just sounded funny."

I explained that there was reason for it to sound funny, that I was actually evading. Something had come up. I had been forced back to my inquiry. I was going to see someone that evening to talk about Adam Swett.

"Oh, for Christ's sake! You promised!"

"I promised that I would take Clare Brinton's advice."

"And?"

"And I am. She said to relax, to be passive, to let the world tell me what I ought to do."

"And?"

"And I read the paper this morning."

"So did I," he said.

"Well, read it again. Read about Edward Curran."

"The guy who jumped?"

"That's right. Read it all, carefully."

"All right, I will. But I don't see . . ."

"You will. And I won't do anything foolish. This is perfectly safe. I promise."

"You're promising a lot these days."

"You seem to be demanding a lot of promises."

"Am I? I'm sorry. No, I'm not sorry. It's just that I care."

"I'm a grownup, Martin. Affection is one thing. Protection is another."

"I guess so," he admitted. "Anyway, good luck."

I thanked him. He promised to call me the next day.

Two

"Why?" she asked. "Why do you want to know? What difference could it possibly make?"

She was not so young as I had expected, and rather heavier than I would have imagined. Lila Swett was slender, had been an elegant woman. Helene Purvis was plump, round-faced, not in any cuddly way . . . But then, perhaps she had let herself go. People can change in a few months. Still, there must have been something that Adam Swett had seen in her. She shook her head, and the gold loops she wore in her ears waved in little arcs.

I explained as much as I thought I had to about Adam Swett's history, or the pieces of it that I knew about. His trail through the offices of doctors and the wards of clinics, the spoor he had left behind him in the files of all these places . . . I told her that I had only recently discovered that my office had been broken into. I wasn't sure, couldn't be positive about it, but I believed that Adam Swett's file might have been the one the burglars were after.

"It's possible," she said. She was sitting on a shapeless upholstered chair, the wine plush discolored at the arms and frayed on one side. She sprawled in the chair, looking as though she had been flung there like the doll of a bored child.

"Oh?"

"There was a lot going on. He was in a hard place. There were militants, and there were bigots who wanted to . . . Well, they both would have been happy to discredit him. White and black. Turn him into an Eagleton. Get rid of him."

"You think it had to do with Harvard?" I asked.

"Why not? That's where he was. That's where all the fighting was. The integrationists, and the separatists, and the white liberals, and the white reactionaries . . . No matter what he did, there was objection from somewhere. And if he didn't do anything, there was objection from everywhere. It was pretty bad."

What she was telling me was not irrelevant. I could see how he might have needed help, mine or Dr. Harney's. Any help he could get.

"Did he ever mention a Dr. Harney to you?"

"Oh, yes. Him. Yes, he mentioned him."

"And?"

"Well, it's a long story."

"I want to hear, if you don't mind telling me."

She thought about it. She got up and crossed the room to the pullman kitchen. "You want a beer?" she asked. I nodded, and she brought back two cans of beer. We popped the tops and drank from the cans.

"It's sort of pointless now," she said. "It's different now. I don't know whether it's better or worse now, but it's different. There was hope then, you know? The raised expectations of the minority groups . . . All that jazz? Now it all seems like it happened on some other planet . . ."

In a circuitous way she told me how it had been, how she had been when she had first met Adam Swett at some organizational evening back when people were still organizing. She was on the fringes of the academic world in Boston, not actually teaching at B.U. but having a couple of courses in their evening division. By the same token, she was rather on the fringes of the black activist world, not being herself political, but being somehow acceptable because of her specialty, which was African music. She had performed that evening, after the discussion, and Adam Swett had introduced himself . . .

"And then it just sort of happened," she said. "We clicked, you know? I guess we managed to fit each other. I didn't demand anything from him, and he didn't demand anything from me. And it was . . . well, relaxing. We started to have lunch together sometimes. And it went on from there. In ways, we were using each other, but everybody uses everybody. He proved to me how I had been right not to get more involved than I was. And I proved to him that there were other things in the world besides angry students and angry faculty and angry communities, and . . . and all that pressure. He could relax.

Or for a while he could. After that, it turned bad. He . . . Well, he was impotent. Hadn't been at the beginning, but later on. That was why he was seeing doctors, I think. Or one of the reasons. You, and then Harney. Harney!"

"Harney?"

"He shot him full of speed. Adam kept saying it was vitamins, but it wasn't any vitamins. I could tell that. And so could he. He knew . . . That was why he went to the clinic in Connecticut. To get off them, to crash. And he was going to—" She broke off.

"He was going to what?"

"I don't know what he was going to do. He talked about a lot of things. He talked about leaving Harvard and going South to some small black school, some place that needed him more than Harvard did. He talked about leaving Lila—that's Mrs. Swett. He talked about a lot of things."

"You never believed him?"

"I don't know whether I believed him or not. For a while I guess I did. I think he was thinking about doing some of them. With me or without me. I don't know. Maybe I don't want to know. He was a good person . . ."

"Did he tell you about himself? His life in Detroit?"

"Oh, he told me. Sure, he told me. Why?"

"I thought about that in connection with my files."

"It's possible. Who cares now?"

"I care. Don't you?"

"What difference does it make whether I care or not? What difference could it possibly make?"

"It could make a difference to you," I suggested.

"Look, I'm not a patient," she said. And then took it back. "I'm sorry. You're right. I know that."

"Why did he go back to Harney?" I asked. "I mean, after the clinic. Why did he go back for more speed? He must have known by then . . ."

"I don't know. I guess maybe he changed his mind. Maybe he needed it. Not for the sex thing. We'd sort of lapsed that way . . . But maybe there was somebody else. Maybe he'd decided to stay and thought he needed it just to get through. I never understood it, though."

"You were angry?"

She took a long pull at the beer, swallowed hard, and then said,

"Of course I was angry. I mean, it wasn't doing him any good. It was hurting him, and he knew it. He'd told me the man was a goddamn pusher. He had a brother, you know, back in Detroit. ODed on shit . . . on heroin . . . when Adam was a boy. You see? It just doesn't make sense!"

She was right. It didn't. On the other hand, people do strange things, make progress and then go back. But she had explained, perhaps, something about Lila Swett's hostility. Or had she?

"What did his wife think about Harney?"

"I don't know. Ask her."

"Or about his leaving Harvard? His going South?"

"She didn't want to go. She didn't want him to go. But then, that figures, doesn't it?"

I thought for a while and sipped the beer. Then I asked, "Do you think he was going back to Harney for treatment? For more shots?"

"Why else go back?"

"I don't know. To tell him off? To threaten him?"

"And that was why he dropped dead? Because he got so angry? No . . ."

I waited. Would she take it the next step? Would she have the confidence in herself to be able to see it? But she didn't. She just shook her head, mourning. There was nothing I could do for her, nothing I could say to her. Not yet, at any rate.

I thanked her for the talk and for the beer.

"That's all right," she said. "I don't mind."

But she did. She minded very much. It was not impossible that the way she looked, the way she sprawled in the chair as if thrown there, the way she had retreated into indifference and apathy all had to do with Adam Swett, whose life and death she minded very much indeed.

I drove back through the sad shabbiness of Somerville, and through the sad shabbiness of Cambridge, too. Aside from a couple of enclaves of money and comfort, and the great bastions of learning, Cambridge is mostly a depressing, depressed place. Not very different, I should think, from the Detroit of Adam Swett's boyhood, young manhood . . . Those of us who are middle class, who were born to the middle class, have learned not to see very much of what is around us. We see, but we filter it out. For Swett, there would have been no such filter. Each boarded-up window, each vacant lot piled with junk, each squalid cityscape must have appeared to him to be beckoning, reminding, threatening. Another kind of pressure to add to those he found waiting for him in his office each day, and those he found in bedrooms at night, his own and Helene Purvis's.

All right, admit it, then. I had failed. I had not inspired whatever trust and confidence he had needed even to start telling me these things. I had been correct, professional, receptive, but that hadn't been enough. Somehow or other, there should have been more, there should have been something better. One can't run after these people, can't tie them down to a chair in the office once they have wandered in. They are free to leave. But when they do leave, still in need, still in pain, our responsibilities are not diminished, only our chances to help.

What I could see now was motive. On both sides, not only on Swett's, as he must have come for one last visit to Harney to denounce, to protest, perhaps to threaten, but also on Harney's side, for Harney must have been frightened or enraged. Swett's anger and Curran's despair were the obverse and reverse of the same coin. And the coin turned out to be the penny they used to put on a dead man's eyes. Enough to go to the police with now?

That would depend, of course, on what the attitude of the police happened to be. If they wanted to pursue the matter, my suspicions would be more than ample. If they wanted to ignore the whole thing, then they could point out—in perfect truth—that I had nothing more than suspicions, no physical evidence of any kind, no fingerprints, no documents, none of the eloquent, mute objects with which crimes on television are generally solved.

So it could go either way. And if they chose to ignore what I was telling them, then I might be in a position of some risk, myself. I could not entirely dismiss the cautions of Martin, whose concern for me could seem smothering sometimes but was nevertheless real. Figure the worst, that Harney had killed Swett, murdered him in cold blood, with premeditation . . . And doctors do that, more often than any other group. They get used to life and death, get too comfortable with mortality, and turn killer, more often, surely, than lawyers, professors, accountants, or any other professional class. There are, after all, risks to Nietzschean thought. If I complained to the police, and they did nothing, and if Harney heard about my complaint, might he not come after me?

A cowardly thing, even to allow such a consideration to weigh in the decision I had to make, but on the other hand, it would have been a foolish, if not a foolhardy, thing not to admit the possibility that there might be risk. The object was to go ahead, but to do so as cautiously and as safely as possible.

In the morning, then, I called Senator Farnsworth and explained to him that I needed to talk to someone, either in the police department or in the district attorney's office, someone he trusted, and someone I could trust. He thought for a moment, and then told me to call Ted Goodman. "He's a bright boy, and I trust him. His father and I were friends. I can call him, if you like, and tell him that you're a friend of mine, and that you'll be calling on him later. Shall I do that?"

"I'd be very grateful. It's a messy business, and I'm a little bit worried by it."

"I understand. And you were right in calling me. I thought it might come down to something like this. And I was anxious, a little, myself. But you'll be all right with Goodman. I can promise you that."

"Thank you."

So he called, and then I called, and I got Goodman's offer to meet me for a drink at the Parker House. "We can talk there as easily as in the office," he said. "And it's so much more pleasant. After all, for a friend of Senator Farnsworth's . . ."

I thanked him. Farnsworth had made the call, and Ted Goodman was telling me that this was the result of the call. The Parker House was not only more pleasant than his office would have been, but safer. No one would see me coming in, wonder what I was doing there, connect whatever Goodman did afterwards with my visit to him. And he was telling me all this without having to say any of it. I liked that, and allowed myself to feel a little bit hopeful. I might be at the end of this whole mess. The prospect of having the burden taken from me was splendid.

After my last patient of the day left me, I started to gather myself together to go to the Parker House. I wondered whether I shouldn't bring Elfinstone's paperback thriller. But there didn't seem to be very much point to it, not without a photograph of the room that would show what he had been describing. And, come to think of it, not even a photograph would show that the room had looked this way before the book had been written and published. Not even that single nub of what I knew to be hard evidence could stand up without the testimony of witnesses who could swear to the fact that the room had looked that way for years, that the objects Elfinstone had described had been there long before the description . . . No, it was a simple question of belief. Either he would believe me or he wouldn't. And I resolved to let it go at that, and to trust to the son of Senator Farnsworth's friend.

Ted Goodman was a tall, attractively disheveled fellow who looked more like a newspaper reporter than like an attorney. He had rather long hair, and wore a rumpled blue suit. The hair kept falling down over his forehead, and he had a habit of flopping it back by tossing his head, both spontaneous and nervous. Boyish, I suppose. And the boyishness was only emphasized by the blue suit. He looked like a schoolboy who had been dressed nicely for prize day, but had played in the yard as hard as ever and now was beginning to think about what his parents would say. Fanciful, of course, but we react to people in these fanciful ways. I hoped the impression he had of me was rather more serious. I tried to be professional, responsible, sane. I asked for a Campari and soda, hoping, I suppose, to further that kind of suggestion. He had a dry martini, up.

The waiter brought the drinks, and Mr. Goodman tossed his hair out of his forehead, raised his eyebrows, and asked me what seemed to be the trouble. "I assume it's some kind of trouble?"

"Yes, I'm afraid so," I said.

"Well, I suppose that's our business, yours as well as mine."

"Trouble and its alleviation."

"I'll drink to that," he said, raising his glass.

We drank to it, and then I told him what I had learned. It took perhaps half an hour. I was as specific as I could be, with names, places, details all clearly and orderly presented as if I were summarizing a case—which, of course, I was. He asked no questions, just listened, nodding from time to time, sipping at his martini, and every once in a while flipping that hair back up onto his head. I concluded with the part about Curran's suicide and my talk with Helene Purvis in Somerville. I explained how it had seemed to Helene—whose final *e* no longer bothered me now that I knew her—that Adam Swett had betrayed her, had betrayed himself, and in going back to Dr. Harney, had gone back on all their hopes. My purpose in this slight detour was to admit a little emotion and humanity into the account, and to enlist, insofar as possible, the sympathies of this young assistant district attorney. I finished by telling him my own theory, all but a certainty now—that Swett had returned to Harney for some confrontation and that there had been what they call in splendid abstraction "foul play."

111

"It's always possible," Goodman said. "Another drink?"

"If you're having one."

He ordered another round. This time there was no toast, no gesture of any kind—not even a toss of the head. The lank forelock hung down over his forehead, untended.

"It's very touchy," he said. "Assuming that what you assume is true, assuming there was a homicide . . . Well, it's a tough case to make. We do them one at a time, you see. And there are good reasons for that. Clouds of suspicion aren't enough. You can't take a little of this and a little of that, and a shadow of another thing, and mix them all together to make guilt. What I mean is that if Elfinstone was involved in the burglary, we'd have to prove it. And then we'd have to prove more connection with Dr. Harney than a doctor-and-patient connection. If there was anything wrong with Curran's suicide, we'd have to prove it, and that'd be very touchy. The mention of Nietzsche is suggestive, but that's all. It's very tough, stirring all this up."

"But there are detectives, aren't there? There is a police force. If a crime has been committed . . ."

"We don't even know that. There has to be probable cause to think a crime has been committed. We usually have something like a dead body with a bullet in it. Hell, most of the time we have not only a body but a man or a woman standing over the body with a gun . . . Five neighbors heard the shouting, heard the shot. There are laws against police harassment. There are requirements for asking for a search warrant, or in this case, maybe, an exhumation. We need evidence to get a body exhumed. If he was buried . . ."

"What do you mean, if?"

"He could have been cremated."

"You mean there isn't anything you can do?" I asked, looking at him as steadily as I could. No anger, no reproach. It does no good, is counterproductive, gets people more resistant than they were to start with.

"Not quite yet. But there might be. There just might be. You could do one more thing, maybe, and that might shift the balance just enough."

"And that would be?"

"Maybe if the medical association investigated this, which they could do if you went to see them, they could turn up something that we might use. Their procedures are quasi-official, and from their hearings we could, well . . . take official notice. Some such start. Or is that asking too much?"

"Not for me," I told him, but I shook my head. "It may be asking too much from them. They're even more cautious than the police are. After all, we're all colleagues. There would have to be at least a complaint from someone with standing. I mean, from a patient, from somebody Harney had treated. Or mistreated . . ."

I broke off. It was a long shot, and yet it was possible. "Maybe if I went back to see Elfinstone . . ."

"That'd be up to you," Goodman said. "I wouldn't."

"You wouldn't? Why not?"

"What do you think he'll do? He'll tell Harney. Harney will just burrow down into his hole, cover his tracks more. Or worse. If he did kill Swett, he's not a nice person, is he? Look, think of it in medical terms. Think of triage. I was in the army, and I had some friends who were army doctors. It's tough, but they had to learn it. To be as useful as they could. You separate out the treatable cases from the untreatable ones. You put your attention and your time where they can help. I do this all the time. We have to. You pick your shots. You work on what you can do. You accept your limitations. You're a doctor. You could be spending this time other ways, helping other people."

"I know," I said. "I've thought of all that. Over and over. It's probably true. It's just that this annoys me. To do nothing would have been intolerable. And once I started, I just kept going, one step at a time."

"And each step of the way, you have to make the decision all over again."

"Yes, that's true."

"Well, maybe this is the last step you ought to take."

"Seeing you," I asked, "or seeing Elfinstone?"

"I meant seeing me. But that's the decision, isn't it?"

"I suppose so."

He signaled to the waiter, making the gesture of writing with one hand on the other palm. I offered to pay for the drinks. He refused. "There's an expense account for this kind of thing," he said. "It was business, after all, wasn't it?"

He might have been telling the truth. I let him pay for the drinks, but I didn't like it.

Three

It would have been better, of course, if there had been no further step even to think about. I had done as much as it was reasonable to do, more probably. And from the ethical standpoint, I had discharged my obligations by talking to Mr. Goodman, laying before him what I had learned and what I had surmised. If the majesty of the Commonwealth of Massachusetts could stand the affront of a possible homicide, so could mine. Right? Of course!

I had no intention whatever of going to see Elfinstone again. It was stupid even to think about it. I found myself, nevertheless, considering the possibilities, working out strategies, figuring the advantages and disadvantages of various kinds of approaches. Convinced as I was that he was on some sort of amphetamine program, I could expect that he would be by now extremely volatile emotionally, would even be exhibiting what is technically called amphetamine paranoia. He had been seeing Harney for some time, and no matter what the controls, what the limitations of the regimen, a couple of years of that kind of stimulation and the effects would be irresistible. That meant, in practical terms, that Elfinstone would be rather more easily manipulable than a normal person. Harney, perhaps, had manipulated him into burglarizing my office. More than probably, there was some sort of manipulation that continued and was still continuing. The interesting thing to think about—just to think about, for I had no actual plans—was the possibility of taking over from Harney as the authority figure, of grabbing the control from Harney and turning Elfinstone against him. That was the kind of daydream I worked up during the next few days, increasingly pleasurable as a daydream, and decreasingly threatening because it was so complicated, so implausible. It would have been nice to turn one of Dr. Harney's creatures against him, then save the creation . . . All very Transylvanian, with the peasants making serpentine lines up toward the castle on the crag, only to have the monster of Dr. Frankenstein join them at the end for their celebration with music and beer steins and laughing children . . . It became distant, recognizable as a daydream, and then began to fade.

Would have faded away entirely, I'm sure, except that John came to town. He had come to New York to participate in some symposium, accepting that invitation, he said, because New York and Boston were not so far apart. He could duck out of New York, whip over to La Guardia, take the shuttle to Logan, and come and see me. It was an unexpected visit. He hadn't known exactly what the schedule would be in New York, whether he would be able to get away, or when, and had left it all hanging, a delightful daydream—his word—until he'd arrived in New York and called me from there. He'd wanted me to come down and join him. I couldn't, not on such short notice. He'd wanted to know if he could come up. He could take the nine o'clock shuttle, get into Boston at ten, and then take the seven o'clock shuttle back the next morning.

"If you want to," I'd said. "It's very . . . strenuous. How about tomorrow night? Couldn't you come up then, and go back from here to Denver?"

He'd hesitated. It had to do with his wife's plans to meet the plane in Denver. How to explain his arrival on a flight that originated in Boston and didn't stop in New York? I told him that all he had to do was take a plane that got in before his original flight was due, and just be there when she got there. Or call from the Denver airport and say he'd caught an earlier plane.

That had convinced him. Which was, actually, strange. He is a competent, practical person, and under any other circumstances, would have been able to negotiate around these problems in logistics and planning. Around me he floundered and fluttered. He said it was love, but it could just as easily have been guilt, or regression. Or a combination of these medically proven ingredients.

At any rate, after all that, he did arrive in Boston, and we went to dinner and then came back to the house. During dinner John was in good spirits, still coming away from the symposium where his appearance had been even more gratifying than the invitation to take

115

part, which had been no inconsiderable distinction. He talked a lot about what Dr. X had said, and how Dr. Y had responded, and how he had come in and turned it around and made them both look a little silly, without even having it look as if he had been making them look silly. Intricate and childish, perhaps, but then, not even psychiatry can escape the penalties of institutionalization—competitive maneuvering, an orientation toward success, the will to triumph. Particularly for men? I asked John whether he didn't think so, too.

"Think what?"

"That maybe you're making more out of it than is good for you? That you shouldn't be taking pleasure in putting other doctors down that way?"

"They were being silly!"

"There are all kinds of ways to deal with silliness. You know that. And I don't care about them, anyway. I care about you. The way you talked about it at dinner . . . You're a man and a doctor, not a barracuda."

"That's sentimental nonsense. Men are killers."

"And women?"

"Women, too. Of course women. Maybe women more than men. All that talk about how the world will be different when women run it? Just foolishness. Look at Mrs. Gandhi, and Mrs. Meir, and Mrs. What's-her-name from Ceylon . . ."

"I see. Well, let's not argue about it," I said, and I poured another glass of brandy into his snifter.

It was a suggestion, and more than a suggestion. A plea? Who knows, now? It was our last best hope. But we didn't drop the argument. It changed, as arguments do sometimes.

John changed the subject to his feelings of imposition at the ways in which he had to treat me, coming up for a sneaky night from New York, worrying about plane connections and not even being able to figure out the way to manage them, himself.

"But I don't feel sneaky. I feel fine. Do you feel sneaky?"

"A little. I guess it's transference," he said.

"Yes, I know."

"I'm sorry."

"I know. But I'm not. I'm glad to see you, that's all."

"Still, I wish it could be better with us. I wish there could be more of us. I feel greedy about you. Want to protect you . . ."

"But, John, that's nonsense," I said, cutting him off. Angry, actually, although perhaps I shouldn't have been. It was not much worse than—not even much different from—his attitude about those other doctors at the symposium. But it affected me more directly. "How can you protect me?" I asked. "You're in Denver and I'm in Cambridge. We're friends and we're lovers, but that's all there is. And it's insulting for you to think that I need protection. I get tired of it. Martin tries to do that sometimes, and I can't stand it."

"All right."

"You're angry," I said, hoping that by bringing it out in the open we could deal with it, get through it.

"And you're not? That was a little hostile, wasn't it? Telling me that?"

"It's true."

"I mean about Martin."

"Well, that's true, too. I mean, why should that be hostile, or why should you be hurt by it. You're married to Arlene. I know that."

"I don't talk about her all the time."

"And I don't talk about Martin 'all the time' either. Only when it's relevant."

"All right, so we're both jerks. Where does that leave you?"

"I didn't say he was a jerk."

"I see. He tries to protect you, and he's not a jerk, but I want to, and that makes me a jerk. Anything else good?"

To placate him, I had to explain. And it was, by this time, a story in which I did not feel much involved, a piece of diverting history. In that spirit, then, I told him about the paperback thriller, and the description of my office, and the whole thing—Elfinstone, Swett, Harney, Curran, Goodman, and all.

He sat there scowling, swirling his brandy but not drinking very often. When I finished, telling him about my daydream of going back to Elfinstone, he looked at me and asked, "And you think I'm crazy, wanting to protect you? Or Martin? Jesus! You are a strange girl!"

"Am I?"

"Yes. Wonderful, but strange. Promise me you won't go near that guy!"

"No."

"Please!"

"Oh, John! Don't say that. Don't . . . 'Please!' never makes any difference. And you don't have the right to ask for that kind of a promise. This is a professional judgment. I'm a grownup. I get to make my own decisions, without consulting you or Martin, or anybody. Or without having to make crazy promises that don't mean anything anyway."

"I'm sorry you feel that way."

"I'm sorry you're sorry," I said.

He sat there, looking at me, not saying anything. I put a record on the phonograph, not that I wanted to hear a record but in order to fill up the silence that sucked at the room. I poured myself a small brandy. We sat pretending to listen to the music, a Brahms quintet, for the first side of the record. I didn't have the heart to play the other side. Instead, I turned the phonograph off and announced, "I'm going to bed."

It was a careful, flat announcement. Not an invitation, but not any prohibition, either. I left the room. I assumed that he would, after a while, follow me. I wasn't at all sure whether I had been at fault. I didn't even know if I wanted him to follow me or not. That would be up to him, I thought. If he did follow, if he swallowed his pride or anger or greediness or whatever, then, maybe . . .

But he didn't. He dozed for a while on the sofa. He left the pillows on the floor. There was his brandy glass on the little oak table. And there was a note under it: "I'm sorry. It isn't working right. My fault, maybe, but that doesn't help. Ever, J."

Not even the full name. An initial. Withdrawal. Or self-effacement.

A great shame, really, and perhaps even a little frightening, for it was a challenge to the assumptions by which I had tried to live. There is such a thing as being too reasonable, too enlightened. One can lose touch with the way the world is, the way people are. I had been supposing, no doubt because I had needed to suppose, that there could be liaisons of friendship, of tenderness, of delight, and even of passion, but not grasping, not trapping, not gnawing at one another . . . Was it an elaborate dream, an invention out of weakness and fear? Or was I right to want this, and unable to find the right man, or the right men? Could I blame the way men are trained and reared and socialized? Did that help—for if all men were socialized that way, I was being unrealistic, fanciful. John had seemed so gentle, so stable, so tranquil. But not even he, not even married and sufficiently supported not to require impossible commitments and foolish pledges, had been comfortable with the limitations I had felt it necessary to impose. My fault, then? My problem? Or were all these questions merely a result of my mood, depressed at having hurt someone, and at having been hurt, myself?

Let it settle a little, I told myself. I put the cushions back on the sofa, and put the brandy snifters away. I had a second cup of coffee, and then went off to the clinic. It was a Saturday morning, and I had a couple of evaluations to do, a diagnostic interview and a conference. I was glad to have work to do, would even have preferred a full day, an overfull day. What was I to do after one, when I left the clinic? Call Martin? Spend the time working out ways not to call Martin? I was getting to be as dependent as they were, and didn't like it.

And it was just as I had feared. The work took my mind off my own situation for a while, closed out all those questions, lifted me up as I exercised judgment, felt competent, paid attention . . . And then left me back where I had been, or even worse, for now there was the prospect of a long afternoon, a long evening, a long night, and then a whole empty Sahara of Sunday to get through. The Museum of Fine Arts? A movie? Nothing wrong with either of them, but that was for kids, for tourists. No, that was unfair, untrue. People who live here go to museums and movies on Sunday. But they have choices. They don't depend, the way I was depending . . .

I decided to take a walk, a long, dumb walk that would maybe make me tired. At least it would do that. At the best, I might find something diverting. An antique? A curio? A book . . . I aimed myself toward Charles Street, a destination about the right distance from the clinic for strenuousness but not exhaustion, and a place where all the possibilities would open up—antiques, brass fittings, and around the corner and up Beacon Street, books, clothes, the world.

A long walk, briskly, does things to the body. The static of the mind dies down and the muscles take over. My shoulders back, my back straight, my calves feeling the reassuring thud of each footfall, I became a machine, an animal, a child. I could look down at the sidewalk just in front of my feet and see the streaming of tiny objects at what appeared to be great speed—the cracks in the sidewalk, gum wrappers, bits of broken glass, a discarded envelope streaking past and under with the distorted energy of close objects one sees from the window of a railroad car. Hypnotic, in a way, and soothing. I had a sense of my size and power, tramping along that way.

It changed at Charles Street. I slowed, dawdled, looked into windows, admired a peculiar cloisonné jug, not Chinese but probably

French in the Chinese manner, and thought about it as a lamp. The right shade and it would be a spectacular lamp. Did I like it enough? There would be the strenuous business of finding a man to wire it and make the shade. And those things are incredibly expensive these days. Eighty, a hundred dollars, or with a teak base even more. And that, after the cost of the jug itself. But it would be a fine lamp. Worth the effort and the money? Should I go in and find out how much they wanted for it?

Be tough! Be reasonable. Okay, it would be a gorgeous lamp—but where? In the living room? In my office? There was a blue in places on the enamel work that looked very close to the blue of my lapis-lazuli horse . . .

And then it all came back. The whole damned thing was with me again, and my rage at John and his behavior, and at Martin's protectiveness, and Ted Goodman's caution, and they combined with the realization that I was on Charles Street, only about four blocks from Elfinstone's apartment. Yes, Virginia, there is a subconscious, and there I was, having walked without knowing why, to the bottom of Beacon Hill, where the question lurked to attract my attention like a bauble in a store window. And through a bauble.

I went into a pastry shop and sat down to have a cup of coffee in order to think. One can't think standing up, not after walking a couple of miles. In fact, the whole point of the exercise had been to avoid thinking, right? And it wasn't working. The decision had to be made, not only about Elfinstone and whether to take that next step, but about what I thought of myself. As a psychiatrist, as a professional person, as a woman, as a human being . . .

Different levels of abstraction will provide different kinds of answers. The professional attitude, clearly, was to let it alone. But was I content to leave it at that, to be no more than the professional? If there is anything to the ideas of liberation, then we cannot compartmentalize ourselves, cannot avoid responsibilities, cannot accept for ourselves the limits of the dreams of others. I was right to hope for a better relationship with John than we had been able to manage. And the failure hadn't been mine. He had been too damned masculine, too dumb, too banal in the ways he had distorted what was clear and obvious and right in front of his big brown eyes in order to fit it all into patterns he had learned long ago, patterns that were not only untrue but useless and even hurtful. Martin, at least, tried from time to time.

But if they were wrong about so basic a thing as how to conduct a love affair with a willing and loving woman, what did that mean about their judgment in other areas? Were they not fitting the realities of professional ethics into the same tight patterns?

To hell with them. The question was simpler than that. The question was merely whether I wanted to go to see Elfinstone or not. And I kind of did. For the possibility of getting a little further along in my pursuit of Harney? In order to have something to go back to Goodman with and therefore to show him that I was serious, was better than the damned district attorney's office and police department put together? Or for the sheer fun of seeing how close my daydream confrontation with Elfinstone would come to the true one? Probably all those things. But mostly because I had allowed myself to wander to within three blocks of his house, because I recognized that my body and at least part of my mind wanted to do it, and because I thought, finally, that if I couldn't trust that kind of an impulse, then I couldn't trust anything.

So I finished my coffee, left the pastry shop, and climbed up Revere Street ("The British are coming!") to Elfinstone's street, Joy.

Four

Having committed myself, I was able to allow myself to feel some apprehension. Would he be home? Would he not be home? Which did I want? If he was out, would I take that as an excuse, as a sign, and drop it? Did the peculiar process by which I had got here mean anything? I decided I wanted him to be home, and I pushed his doorbell with a long, firm push, as if doorbells were like piano keys and could produce different tones according to the touch one applied. The buzzer answered. I let myself in through the inner door.

I found him standing in his doorway, looking down the stairs to see who was coming to see him. He furrowed his brow, trying to remember me.

"Dr. Chayse," I reminded him. "You remember me?"

"Oh, yes, yes. The one with the office."

"That's right. I'm sorry to bother you again, but I think there are things we ought to discuss . . ."

"Oh, God! Now?"

"There are matters of some importance . . ."

"Always," he said, looking pained. He also looked in need of a shave. And even thinner than I remembered him.

"May I come in for a little while?" I asked, almost little-girlish.

"Yeah, why not. Sure." He stood aside and allowed me to enter his apartment. He sat down behind his desk, the good Chinese Chippendale desk I remembered from my earlier visit, and put his chin in his palms and his elbows on the desk. I moved a side chair to face him across the desk and sat directly in front of him. He was not going to use the desk to hide from me, to ward me off.

"What can I do for you, Dr. Chayse?" he asked, rather more crisp and assured than he had been at the door.

"You can tell me the truth this time," I said. "Not for my sake, but for your own."

"Ah, I see. An appeal to my self-interest. Or do you appeal to my concern for my soul?"

"Does the one exclude the other?" I asked.

"They don't always coincide," he said, smiling—not so much at his remark, I thought, but at the epigrammatic style into which we had somehow fallen. He enjoyed it, liked to think of himself as feeling natural in that clipped, witty, semi-abstract manner.

"No," I said, "they don't. But there are questions that come up sometimes of sufficient importance to involve both self-interest and the soul. Do you know very much about Dr. Harney?"

He didn't startle. And I couldn't tell whether it was by an exercise in self-control or not. On the other hand, he did not answer immediately, either. He just sat there, looking at me, probably thinking. I didn't want to give him the chance to do much of that. Having the feeling that I'd scored a little, I wanted to follow it up.

"I know about the reason for the break-in. I know more about it, perhaps, than you do. I can't think that he would have told you everything."

"Who is Dr. Harney?" he asked, but it was too late. A few seconds sooner and it would have been an attack. Now it was a retreat. He didn't even believe that I would believe his question.

"That's not a serious question, is it?" I asked.

"Sure it is. Why shouldn't it be?"

"The name of your doctor has slipped your mind? The man you depend on most in the world?"

"You're guessing. You're imagining things. You're fishing . . ."

"I almost wish I were," I said. "But I'm not and you know I'm not."

He opened his mouth as if to speak, then closed it. He reached down under the desk, and I felt a tremor of fear. What would he come up with? A gun? A knife? A baseball bat? He produced a package of cigarettes and a book of matches. He lit a cigarette, stalling for time. Also needing the cigarette. Both were good signs, or good for me.

"Why have you come here?" he asked. "What is it that you want?"

"I want to help you," I said.

"Sure. Of course you do."

"You don't believe me," I said. "It's still the truth. I have nothing against you."

"You think I broke into your office, don't you?"

"It wasn't your idea. You didn't even want to do it. You were forced to."

"Look, I'm not admitting anything. I'm not saying anything at all. I'm asking what you want."

"And I'm telling you. I want to help you."

"Are you wired?"

"Am I what?"

"You have a tape recorder in your bag, or something like that?"

"No. Nothing like that," I said. I opened my bag and showed him. "See? Nothing." But it was another good sign. Amphetamine paranoia—if he was lucky. Otherwise, strike the qualifying adjective.

"Then what's the point of all this? Last time you came with questions. This time you've got answers. Whether they're true or not, you've got them. And I don't want help."

"Don't you? You like being junked up all the time? That makes you feel good? You like being twenty pounds underweight, and unable to sleep, and either racing or crashing? You like being Dr. Harney's creature?"

"I don't know what you're talking about."

"You do. You don't want to admit it to me. And perhaps you shouldn't. Not until you trust me a little more . . ."

"Why should I trust you? You walk in off the street like this? I don't know you!"

"You know my office. You've been there. You know that I'm a doctor. And while you're right not to trust all doctors, maybe you've been trusting the wrong one."

"I don't think we have anything to talk about," he said, trying that elegant smile again, but it was a poor copy.

"Let me put a hypothetical case to you," I suggested. "A sort of plot. You know about plots. You do write mysteries. And other books as well . . . Let's talk shop for a little, all right?"

He sighed. "Talk," he said. He put the cigarette out, stubbing it out with an energy that showed his frustration, his anger. He was killing the cigarette.

"Let's assume that there's a doctor who is treating patients with amphetamines. Nothing illegal about it, but ethically close to the line.

Possible trouble with the medical association. Possible trouble of other kinds if one of his patients gets angry enough. And one of his patients does get angry. What is the doctor to do?" I paused, and waited for an answer.

"I don't know. What?"

"Let's make it a thriller. Why not have the doctor kill the patient?"

"Why not? It's your plot."

"It may be our plot, but you'll see. It will connect soon enough. One of the things he has to worry about, either before he kills the patient when he's trying to get some handle on him, or afterwards, when he's trying to cover his tracks, is what the patient said to other doctors. To a psychiatrist the patient had been seeing. And so he needs to burgle the files of the psychiatrist. He can't afford to take the risk, himself, but he doesn't have to. He has a whole lot of patients, after all. And they all depend on him. Because without the shots, without the amphetamine, they crash, and they feel terrible for days, can't work, can't function. And that means that he can get them to do all kinds of things for him. Just by asking, you see, because there's always that threat. So he asks one of his patients who writes mysteries . . ."

I paused again. There could be a question. A reaction. I didn't want to get too specific or particular, because I didn't want Elfinstone to know exactly what I did and didn't know. I needed any clues I could get as to what direction to go.

"It seems to me just a little fanciful," he said.

"Is it?"

"Look, Dr. . . ."

"Chayse. Sarah Chayse."

"Okay, Dr. Chayse. What do you expect me to say?"

"I don't expect you to say anything. I want you to understand that I'm telling you the truth. That I understand what has happened. That I realize that you need help. What happened to my patient could happen to you."

"What happened to your patient?"

"He's dead. He was killed."

"Who was he?"

"I can't tell you that."

"No, of course not," he said sarcastically.

"It wasn't Curran."

"Who's Curran?"

"The man who jumped off the Hancock Building last week. Another one of Dr. Harney's patients."

"You think Harney pushed him off the building?"

"Not directly. Harney pushed him, maybe. But not off the building. He jumped off the building. My patient died in Harney's office. And Harney signed the death certificate."

"What does that prove?"

"Prove? I'm not sure that it proves anything. Not all by itself. But this was the man whose files you tried to get in my office. You know who it is, don't you?"

"I don't know anything."

"You don't know, but you worry. You worry about whether there is a way out. And there is. I can help you."

"What was the name? Never mind all that shit with medical ethics. Either I recognize a name, or I don't. Either you're telling me something real, or you're making up a whole line of garbage. I don't know what to think. Is there a name? Tell me!"

"I can't tell you the names of any of my patients," I said. "But that shouldn't put you into a sweat, should it? Not much of a sweat, anyway . . ."

He sagged a little. Nothing dramatic, nothing like what an actor would do in a film. But there were minor adjustments in the way he sat, a shift in weight, so that very slowly the palms of his hands, which had been supporting his chin, moved along the jaw, and as his head settled, it came to rest with the little hollow below the ears and in front of the mastoid bone settled into that cradle his hands still made. It was a slow, entirely unconscious change. I had won, the first round anyway.

"Tell me about yourself," I said.

"What's the use?"

"What I told you at the beginning is still true. I want to help you. We can help each other."

"I knew there was a catch. There always is."

"No catch. No matter what you do, whether you help me or not, I want to help you. No catch at all."

"No, nothing like that."

"You don't have to do anything you don't want to do."

"Never. Why should I have to do anything?"

"Why should you have had to do anything? Why should he have made you do things you didn't want to do?"

126

"People do. They enjoy it. That's what I can't figure about you. It's some kind of a power trip. Got to be."

"No. It's just that I don't like to see people pushed around. And there isn't anything I can do for my patient any more. But there are ways I can make up for it, helping you. And if I help you, maybe you'll want to help me. Not have to but want to."

"Right away. Boy scouts and girl scouts, helping each other across the goddamn street!"

"Nobody has ever helped you? You've never helped anyone? I can't believe that."

"Okay, don't. I don't care what you believe. You can believe that for every goddamn drop of rain that falls a flower grows, if it makes you happy."

"You're very bitter, aren't you? Why?"

"It is to laugh! I guess I just have a rotten disposition, that's all. I've been divorced twice. My first wife ran off with a saxophone player . . . Would you believe? Just like in the goddamn movies! My second wife hit me worse. She didn't run off with anyone. She just couldn't stand me. Threw my ass out of the house. So with alimony and child support and back taxes and premiums on the insurance policies I have to keep up, I have a nut of forty grand a year before I can buy myself a fucking peanut-butter sandwich. And I made it for a while. Kept my damned head up. Wrote five books a year . . . For two years, I did that. And then I just couldn't do it any more. Couldn't. So I got some help. And now I write more than ever, but it's all rotten, and earns dogshit, and I'm further behind every month, every week, every hour . . ."

"And that was why you went to Harney?"

"No, dear, I went to Harney for fun. I thought a little speed would help me listen to music better." He looked up at me and smiled at his terrible joke. It was a self-conscious, woebegone smile, but it was as brave as he could muster. And for the first time I liked him a little. Not for the suffering, but for the bravery of that smile, of the gesture of standing aside a little and trying to be something other than the suffering.

"It hasn't helped, has it?"

"For a while it helped. Now I need it just to keep going. And I need Harney. And he knows it."

"You don't need Harney. You need other kinds of help. You need to . . ."

"I need to get my hands on thirty thousand dollars is what I need. And I'm not going to do that spending six weeks in a clinic. Or six days. And that's assuming the fucking clinic is free. You know of clinics with scholarships? Room, board, tuition, medical bills, and thirty grand of spending money? You know of any, you write the name on a piece of paper, and . . . Oh, shit!"

"You can't like yourself the way you are."

"I have a choice?"

"Of course you do. That's what I'm trying to tell you. I can help you. What one doctor can do, another doctor can do, but in other ways, and with other objectives in mind."

"Sure."

"You're not convinced?"

"Not really. It'd be nice, but no, not really. What if everything you're saying is true? What if it's all just the way you lay it out? What then? So you help me, you get me all cleaned out and rehabilitated, and the rest of it. A new man, with a bounce in my step and a twinkle in my eye, lead in my pencil and love in my heart . . . Then what? If I remember your damned plot, the other doctor comes and kills me, right?"

"I don't think so."

"Oh, that's fine. I feel a whole lot better. But what if you're wrong?"

"Let's assume it's a risk. Not a great risk, but a risk. Some things are worth risk, aren't they? You want to go on this way?"

He didn't answer. I thought about what he had said in his bright patter, and tried another tack. "What about your sex life?"

"What sex life? If I could afford one, which I can't, there still wouldn't be any sex life. I don't even remember what it is that people do any more."

"All right, then, if I just get up and walk out? If we leave things this way—just the way things are? That's all right with you?" I got up.

"Oh, cut it out. Sit down. You think I'm fooled? I'm not fooled. I know a ploy when I see one. But sit down anyway."

I sat down again. It didn't matter what the terms were. He'd asked me to sit, asked me to stay, asked me at least to discuss what there was that we could do. It was a start.

"What do you want me to do?" he asked, lighting another cigarette.

"Whatever you want to do. I want to help you."

"Yeah, and you want me to help you. Or you want me to want to help you, which is one of those semi-meaningless constructions."

"There is meaning in it. There can be."

"Not with me. I'm not likely to be much help. I ought to warn you about that, you know. I'm all piss and wind lately, and nothing to me. Nothing left. I'm a fucking weakling."

"It takes a certain amount of strength even to admit that as a starting place."

"And every cloud has its silver lining, right?"

"Have you been this honest with anyone this week? This month?"

"No."

"Well, how does it feel?"

"It feels like shit. Don't you think I have any pride? I used to be—" He broke off.

"You used to be?"

"I used to be a lot of things," he said.

"Such as?"

He told me about himself, about his youth and his young manhood. Deerfield, Princeton, a couple of years at *Time,* a few short stories in the magazines, a book contract, a novel, good reviews, a second novel, and then, for no reason, it all fell apart. His family, his work, his second family, his life . . .

"Some people know how to bounce back, you know? And I used to. But after a while tennis balls go dead. They just don't bounce any more. They lie there looking dirty, and kids play with them, and then finally dogs chew them up. When I was a kid we had a dog that loved to chew up tennis balls. A golden retriever. Named Harcourt, for God's sake . . . Is that what you want to hear, Doctor? About my golden retriever?"

"Maybe. If it's important. We'll get to it if it's important. Otherwise it's a joke, isn't it? And if it is, we get to the joke and talk about that."

"A joke, yes. Little girl psychiatrist and little boy writer will go out and catch the big bad man . . . Dr. Chayse, you're in worse shape than I am!"

"You've been reading too many paperback thrillers," I told him.

"As Disraeli said, when somebody asked him if he'd read George Eliot's new book, 'When I feel like reading a novel, I write one.'"

"Would you consider this—another plot?"

"I could *plotz* with your plots. Show-biz talk, which is to say, Yiddish."

He was resisting, but he was afraid. But so was I. I would have preferred another, and certainly a stronger, person to send off on such an errand. But I had no choice. And neither did he, for that matter.

"What I have in mind is that we could go to the medical association. That would be safe and discreet. No risk."

"Terrific. Go. What do you need me for?"

"Blood tests. You go to Dr. Harney whenever your next appointment is. You behave exactly the way you always behave. Take the same shots. Absolutely the same thing as you would do anyway. Except that you let me know when you're going, and right after you leave him, you come to a hospital. I'll meet you there. We'll draw a little blood, and the analysis will be presented to the medical association. That'd be a start . . ."

"That's a wonderful idea, really fine. You got any more wonderful ideas like that? Because either you're wrong about Harney and he's harmless, or you're right and we're both going to wind up dead. If that's true . . . What do you think the medical association has? Cops? They'll issue a reprimand! They'll hold hearings. They'll have committees consider. It takes a while, you know. And he'll know where they got the blood. And who put me up to it."

"Has he ever told you exactly what he was injecting you with?"

"He didn't have to tell me."

"But did he?"

"I don't remember. I don't think so, no."

"Well, don't you think we ought to find out? If I'm going to help you?"

"It's still my ass in the sling."

"No, I promise you. He'll never know. He won't have any way of finding out."

"He'll know about you, won't he? And where do you think he'll figure you got the analysis, the blood, the body? Got to be me!"

"If I can arrange for police protection for you? Would that change your mind?"

"I don't know. It's not that easy to get police protection. And they don't keep it up for very long. There are more murders in Boston these days than in Chicago. The cops are busy enough with the Mafia. And with collecting from the bookies and the numbers people."

"I have connections," I said. "If I can get something worked out so that you're safe, so that you're satisfied you'll be safe . . . Then would you do it?"

130

"I'll think about it. Let me know what the deal is, what the arrangement is, and I'll think about it."

"All right," I said. "That's fair enough. And what can I do for you? How can I help you? You want my help?"

"Let me think about that, too. You start helping me, get me cleaned up, all the rest of it . . . what happens? I stop going to see Harney, stop coming by for my shots. What the hell do you think he's going to think? That I've become a Christian Scientist? Joined Amphetamines Anonymous? Moved to Milwaukee? Come on!"

"All right," I said. "That's for you to decide. And you may be right. We have to think about Harney. Then we can think about you."

"Yeah, we have to think about Harney. We sure as hell have to think about him. I think about him a lot, you know?"

"Yes," I said. "I know."

"Yeah, you know!"

I got up. I looked at him, wondering which way he'd jump. But he didn't jump. He just sat there.

"I'll call you," I said.

"Yes, you do that. You call me, any time of the day or night. We never sleep. Not when we're souped, we don't. We sit here and write shit for shitty people to read so I can send shitty alimony to my shitty wife and shitty taxes to my shitty government. You going to fix all that too?"

"We could try," I said.

I left. It had been hopeful there for a while. And there was still a chance. It would depend on his mood, on how badly off he was, how badly he thought of himself. But I had at least tried. And I wasn't sorry. John, Martin, all of them had been wrong. I was sure of that.

I had been right to try.

Five

Certainties fade. It was late that night, in that free-floating time between going to bed and drifting off to sleep, that I began to reconsider the events of the afternoon, the interview with poor Charles Elfinstone, and how neatly it had coincided with my earlier daydreams. It was, in one way, enormously satisfying, but there was also something a little disturbing about it. Too pat, too simple. Or, more specifically, I wondered whether I had listened hard enough and openly enough. I had accused John in my mental courtroom of bending and distorting reality to conform it to his preconceptions, much to his cost and to my own. Hadn't I also done the same thing with Elfinstone? Had I considered his reluctance, his fear, his . . . well, his rights? He hadn't volunteered to be treated by me. He certainly hadn't volunteered to join my crusade to expose Dr. Harney. And obviously Elfinstone was in fragile shape.

Still, we make such decisions all the time. Surgeons do most vividly, but they occur in all areas of medicine. It's nice when a patient comes in with one ailment, one discreet problem, and the rest of the body and the mind are entirely sound. Then one can cut, medicate, treat . . . Most of the time it is a matter of playing one weakness off against another, of figuring the needs and the odds of risk. I could tell myself that, could convince myself that the prognosis for Elfinstone was not very good when I came into his life, or when he came into mine. Still, I was meddling, was therefore responsible, and I could not help but wonder how he would stand up to the strain. Should I have been a little slower, tried to think of other instrumentalities that might have accomplished the same purpose with fewer side effects, with less pressure on his shaky self-esteem?

But what was the use? It was too late to do it differently now. And to call Elfinstone and revise the plan would be to seem less than monolithically secure. What strength he had, if he had any, he derived from others. I needed him to derive a lot from me, at least for a little while. To call him now would be to ruin everything. So, with an act of will, I turned my thoughts away from him, thought for a while about John, got to the point where I was ready to put the blame on him for my decision to go back to Elfinstone, then decided that was ridiculous. Martin? Clare Brinton? That cloisonné pot? I tried to remember the details of that pot, the colors, the flaring out and drawing in, and the way the handles sprouted up out of the design . . . And fell asleep.

The next day I felt rather better about it. Elfinstone was not, after all, obliged to do anything. He could forget it. He could refuse to have anything further to do with me, and I could let him know that that was all right, reassure him, offer to be of any help I could any time he felt the need of it, and let him off the hook. If that was what he wanted. But he didn't want that. He called. Which was, I thought, a splendid sign. I had told him I would call him. But he called me. And said that he would be seeing Harney the next day, Monday. "All I'm agreeing to do is come by for a blood test, you understand," he said.

"That's all you have to do."

"After that, if I want to drop it, I can drop it?"

"Any time."

"All right, then, what hospital?"

I told him to come to the clinic. A technician could draw the blood there, and it would be sent out to a lab. There wouldn't even be a name on the sample. Just a number.

"Okay, and then? What happens then?"

"Then we'll talk. I'll see about getting help for you. It could all work out at the same time. You could check into the clinic for a few days—just for safety."

"Your clinic?"

"It isn't mine. I work there."

"I mean, the clinic where you work?"

"Or another. You don't even have to use your real name. We'll work it out. I promise."

"Yeah," he said. Doubting and hoping at the same time.

"You're doing the right thing," I said. "For yourself."

"Sure, sure."

"What time, then?" I asked.

"I don't know. It ought to be somewhere around two. Maybe a little after. Depending on traffic."

"I'll be waiting for you."

"Yeah, you do that. See you."

"See you tomorrow," I said, and felt fine. It was, after all, what he had wanted, himself. It was a chance out of the mess he'd been locked into for years. And there was enough left of him so that he was able to take it. He'd have a good chance of coming back. Second, third, and fourth thoughts notwithstanding, I had been right all along, right from the start.

I spent a nice quiet Sunday reading the Boston *Globe* and the New York *Times,* catching up on the work I had let slide while running around on this Harney thing, reading journals, looking at notes on cases, even writing a little in the afternoon, working on the rough notes for a paper I'd been thinking about. Even without John, there were still conferences, and I could go to them the way ordinary doctors did, for the ordinary reasons. Certainly I would not let the collapse of that relationship exclude me from conferences. Certainly not! In all kinds of ways, I was feeling better about myself. I went out to see a double bill of old Carmen Miranda movies at the Orson Welles, and had an onion and pepper pizza, and didn't feel like a waif or a stray—just a single woman doing what I pleased. And I took a bath, did the double-crostic in the tub, and then fed the cat and went to bed, feeling good about the day before, tranquil about the day that was ending, and confident about the one to come.

But he didn't call. He didn't show up and he didn't call. I had canceled my first two appointments at home, and I was waiting at the clinic for him, waited past two-thirty, past three, called his home, got no answer, called my home and told Stanley to cancel the rest of the day for me, and then sat there not knowing what else to do. I waited until four, then gave up. No Elfinstone, no message, nothing. I drove by his apartment on Joy Street, rang the bell, got no answer, got back into the car and drove home.

All kinds of possible explanations, but I didn't believe any of them. Of course, logically, he could have been hit by a bus, could have tripped over a loose piece of pavement and broken an ankle, could have been mugged . . . But not today. Not in a coincidence of such grotesque neatness. But what other explanation was there? He didn't have to say anything to Harney, didn't have to do anything, only be himself, be what he always was, behave exactly as he had always behaved. Not difficult!

Fine, except that he hadn't shown up at the clinic. He hadn't called. He had to be somewhere. What I wanted to do was to call Dr. Harney, but . . .

Or was it? I didn't have to be me. I could be anyone I wanted. But who would be calling Charles Elfinstone? Who would call him at his doctor's office? One of his ex-wives? I hadn't any idea what their names were. And Harney might know. So, someone else. A publisher? His agent? One of those women from Master Artists Corporation? Why not? It was not, perhaps, overwhelmingly convincing, but neither could there be any way of exposing it. The worst that could happen would be that I would get nowhere, and that's where I was anyway.

I called Harney, dialing the number and working up a nasalized variation of my own voice that would be neither instantly recognizable nor obviously grotesque. Just a little distortion. "Dr. Harney? Dr. Harney, this is Miss Walters at Master Artists. In New York?" I liked the interrogative inflection on "In New York."

I liked it, but I never got to use it. What is the point in putting on an accent, or a persona of any kind, if you are talking to an answerphone machine. The machine announced that Dr. Harney was not in the office, that the caller should leave a number and that someone would return the call at the earliest possible moment. Wait for the tone and speak slowly and clearly, please . . .

At ten of five? What happened to the receptionist? For that, too, there were possible explanations. She sick, and he called away on some emergency. And Elfinstone with a broken ankle somewhere, all of them innocent, unrelated happenings? I hardly thought so. I tried Elfinstone's number again, and again got no answer.

I called Ted Goodman, told him what I had done, what Elfinstone had said he would do, and that Elfinstone had disappeared.

"Well, maybe, he might have."

"What else could have happened to him?"

"He could have changed his mind. He could have gone to a movie. He could be in a bar, nursing a beer. He could be anywhere."

"Couldn't you look for him? I'm worried about him. I feel responsible."

"Yes, I can see that," he agreed. He was being polite, but just barely, and he was allowing his effort to show.

"Isn't there anything you can do?"

"Tonight? Not really. Keep calling him. If he's not back by morning, if you haven't heard from him and can't find him, then . . ."

"Then?"

"Well, I guess I could go talk to Harney. I can go over to ask about Curran. It's as good an excuse as I need, I suppose. At least I'll have a chance to look around. I could even ask about Elfinstone."

"Not until morning?"

"What if Harney has gone to a motel with his receptionist? Maybe Monday night is their night. Maybe her husband works late in the store on Monday night, or wherever he works. So that's what they do on Mondays. And Elfinstone is scared out of his mind and is hiding in a movie in the combat zone . . . What if that's all that's happened? How do you think I'm going to look if I put the bulls on them? Be reasonable. Either your guy is alive or he isn't. And if he's alive now, he'll be alive in the morning. And if he isn't, then it can wait. Right?"

"Yes, you're right. I'm sorry. I'm being a pest . . ."

"Only a little. I'm glad you called. I'll hear from you in the morning?"

"Either way," I promised.

No, it wasn't right. Correct maybe, but not right. In any event, there had been no way for me to argue with him, nothing for me to say. He was being helpful, as helpful as he could afford to be. More than he would have been to somebody else? Yes. But still, not enough.

What the hell could have happened to that stupid Elfinstone? The choice was easy enough. Go and do what he had said he would do. Or not. And if not, then call. A telephone call, just to say he'd changed his mind. Was that so much to ask? Not of a normal person maybe, but then, Elfinstone was shreddy, had been shredding for years . . .

"What's the matter?"

Stanley had come in. He stood there, not wanting to intrude, but not wanting to ignore what my posture, my expression must have been broadcasting.

"I don't know," I said. "Nothing, I hope."

"Well, if that's how it is when nothing's the matter, I hope you don't have any grief come into your life. You want some coffee?"

"No, thanks. Sit down for a minute. Tell me I'm not crazy."

He sat down. He said, "You're not crazy."

"No, listen first. Then tell me . . ."

"Tell you what? That you're not crazy? Or what I think? Do I get to think?"

"Please!"

He nodded. I told him about my meeting with Elfinstone, the arrangement we'd made, the call on Sunday from Elfinstone to me, and then what had happened, or hadn't happened, earlier during the day. No word. No Elfinstone, no doctor, no receptionist. And not much help from Goodman, either. I explained what Goodman had said, and how it was possible that all these things could be explained. But I didn't feel good about it.

"Okay, then," he said. "You're not crazy. You could be wrong maybe, but you're not crazy."

"How could I be wrong?"

"It could be what Goodman said. I hope so. You hope so too!"

"Yes, I guess I do," I said. "Was I wrong? To go to Elfinstone that way?"

"Right? Wrong? Do those words mean anything? It works or it doesn't work. Isn't that so?"

"I guess."

He sat for a moment, thinking. Then he cleared his throat. "You want me to stay here with you? It might be a good idea. What do you think?"

I thought about it. It was a generous offer, perhaps even more generous from Stanley than it might have been from someone else. He could have been self-conscious about the idea of offering himself as the big black buck to protect the white missy . . . Some such garbage as that. And I could have been less self-conscious than I was. Or I ought to have been. It wasn't the blackness but the maleness that got to me. The same kind of patronizing that had bothered me in John and in Martin, and in other ways, in other men for years. Roger and I could have worked everything else out, could have saved the marriage—maybe—if he hadn't been the same way. In spades! (An unfortunate association, the question being Stanley's offer . . .)

137

"It wouldn't be much of a bother," he said.

And I liked the accuracy of his locution. Not "no bother" which would have been a lie, but the homely truth. I was tempted to accept. And yet, to have done so would have been to admit my own fears, their scale, their power. If I didn't admit to myself that I was scared, then maybe I wasn't scared. And if I wasn't scared, then maybe there was nothing to be scared of. Primitive logic, but we are all primitive beings in the crunch.

"No, I'll be all right. I'm sure it's all nerves and foolishness. Nothing's going to happen to me."

"Nothing happened to Swett?"

"I don't know any more. I really don't."

"Elfinstone never broke in here?"

"He never said so, never admitted it in so many words."

"Okay, then I change my mind. You're crazy. Crazy as a bedbug. But I'll still stay here if you want me to. We can make wallets and weave baskets together."

"No, Stanley. It's a kind offer. And I do appreciate it. If I were really worried, I'd just leave the house. I'd go to a hotel or something. Nothing easier. But I'm not. And I don't want to be protected . . ."

"Okay. You're the doctor."

"You keep saying that."

"I have to keep reminding myself. It gets more and more difficult to believe."

"Thanks."

So Stanley left. And of course, as soon as he'd gone, I regretted having sent him away. Still, to run after him and call him back would have been not only to admit but to underline my fears. To admit them not only to myself but to him. I thought of it, but couldn't do it. Or wouldn't. I called Elfinstone's number instead. Maybe the bum was back from his thrilling triple-feature triple-X festival by now. If he was, he wasn't answering his phone.

A stiff gin on the rocks, and I felt a little better. I turned on the television set to watch the local news. Maybe there had been a lunatic running amok on the MBTA, killing eleven and wounding twenty-two, one of whom would turn out to be Charles Elfinstone . . .

There were wrangles on the school committee, and rage from the mayor's office, and high-toned scorn from the governor about issues that were ten years old and looked to be good for another ten. Not the kind of thing the newscasters would put up over a mass murder

. . . Figure the broken ankle, then? Or the movies? Still in the movies? Was that possible? Or he could have gone from the movie theater to a restaurant. Or maybe he was hiding in the movies . . . Hiding not only from Harney, but also from me. Hiding, therefore, from himself. Not implausible.

But then the phone rang. It was about time! I caught it on the second ring.

"Hello?"

Nothing. A bad connection?

"Hello? Who is this?"

Nothing. A breather? Or Elfinstone, working up his nerve to say something? Or . . . Harney?

I hung up. I waited a couple of minutes. It could have been a bad connection. In which case, whoever had called would call back. But it could have been anything. I had no idea. Harmless child playing with a telephone, dialing numbers at random, perhaps from Kansas City or Sante Fe . . . Or a Boston pervert? Or Elfinstone or Harney. No way to tell. I thought about putting down my drink, getting a toothbrush, and leaving the house. Enough reason yet? I didn't think so. If it came down to it, I might. There were other ways to handle it.

I called Stanley. He wasn't home yet. I called Martin, got his service, asked for them to page him and have him call me, and they said they would. I hung up and waited while they sent a radio signal out that made the beeper in his belt go off so that he would call them so they could tell him to call me. A complicated process, but it works more or less. It took four minutes. I was furious with myself for having stared at my watch, for having actually timed it, but what else was there to do? Yes, I was ready to admit that I was getting a little bit nervous. I was ready, anyway, to admit it to myself. Not necessarily to Martin.

"Sarah? What's up?"

"Thinking about you, that's all. Can you come over?"

"Now? I'm having dinner with the people from Vauxhall." Vauxhall was a systems analysis firm specializing in medical economics, based in Dallas but with fantastic connections in Washington. I had forgotten that this was the night he was to meet with them.

"Of course not now," I said. "I mean after. I was wondering how it was going. And feeling guilty. I should have told you before, but obviously, when you're done with them come over. We can celebrate together if it's good, or mourn together if it's bad. Or speculate together if you can't tell. That's . . . that's why I called. Also, I thought it would look good for them to see how important you are, with people beeping your beeper."

"Sarah? You are . . . you're just wonderful. And yes, of course I'll be over. That's just the damndest, nicest thing . . . And it will be fine. With you thinking about me, how can it not be? How could it be anything else?"

"Well, think of me too, then."

"I will," he said. "And I'll see you later on. Ten-thirty. Eleven."

"That'll be fine. Luck," I said, and hung up.

That cut it down a lot. Four hours or so? I could get through four hours. And then Martin would be with me. Not out of panic or unreasonable fear, but for perfectly healthy, sane, delightful reasons. Four hours was not so hard to get through.

I went off to fix myself a rarebit. And to open a bottle of white wine. I turned on the television set and had dinner to the network news. I must have finished cleaning up the kitchen a little before eight. I put a bottle of champagne in the refrigerator, just in case Martin had a triumph to report, and could get his funding for his emergency service . . .

And then I heard the sound of the glass breaking.

Six

I hesitated. If I hadn't, perhaps I might have got to the kitchen door, got out, got away. But at the moment I had to decide whether to go toward the noise, stay where I was and try to hide, or flee. In fact, I froze for a moment, feeling the three impulses conflicting not so much in my mind as in the muscles of my calves and thighs. In a process of quite brief duration in real time but terribly slow in psychological time, I considered the significance of what I had heard, remembered the glass panes that flanked the oak front door, figured out that nothing else, nothing inside the house, could have made such a sound. It took a while for my mind to come to some decision and then to inform my leg muscles. Then I started toward the kitchen door, but it may not even have been that way. It might not have been so conscious as that. It is altogether possible that the sound of footsteps, light, muffled, deliberately stealthy, registered somehow, and that my reaction to them was to try to flee. I took only a couple of steps before I saw him.

It was Dr. Harney. He was wearing a black raincoat and a black hat. He was wearing gloves. He was wearing a gun in his right hand.

Wearing a gun? You see how slow it was, how strange, how difficult to adjust to the strangeness! Even after the vague apprehension, after the more particular uncertainty I'd felt as a result of the telephone call, I was still unprepared for anything so crude as a man with a gun standing there in the hallway.

"Don't move, Dr. Chayse."

"How crude, Dr. Harney."

"Is it? Only on the surface. It is intended to be crude, to appear as

141

crude as any burglar would be. Or as one of your patients trying to appear to be a burglar. Crude, but not without some thought, some wit."

"Oh," I said. "I see. That makes it all right."

"I am happy you see it that way," he said.

The formality of the exchange, the deliberate edge of wit, worked to allow me a chance to regain some minimal composure. Not as much as I might have liked, certainly not with a gun pointed at me . . . but still, enough to say, "You don't really want to do this, do you?"

"Ah, you're being professional, eh? We fall back on what has worked in the past. That's right, isn't it? Well, just remember that works both ways. For me, too. And it does not seem encouraging for you. The prognosis is not good."

"Why did you kill Swett?"

"He was crazy. He turned on me. I had helped him, had done for him exactly what he wanted me to do. And then he changed his mind, and he blamed me. Not fair. Squashy and cheap and sentimental. He deserved worse than he got. He deserved more pain . . . It was very quick."

"He was not a true Nietzschean?"

"He told you about Nietzsche?"

"Indirectly. I didn't pick it up, didn't understand what he meant by it, or how he meant it, until I saw it again. In Mr. Curran's suicide note."

"I have been caught out, then. In errors of judgment about people. Regrettable. But the theory still holds good. I still believe it. And it is to protect that theory, and my practice, and those others of my patients who rely upon that theory and that practice, and upon me, that I am forced to do this. There is no rancor. I want you to understand that. Nothing personal."

"Would you like to sit down?"

"So we can talk? So you can try to talk me out of pulling the trigger? Save yourself the trouble. There is no point. It's a false hope."

"Still, there are questions. There are some things that puzzle me."

"Isn't that a shame!"

"In a way, yes. I assume that you were as open with these other patients as you were with me when I came to see you. Were you?"

"Oh, yes. I have my code of ethics. Not, perhaps, a code you would share, but a code. And demanding. I believe it . . ."

142

"Then what do you do at the end of the spurt? These people you treat, they may have three years? Five? But then what happens?"

"They burn out."

"And you can live with that?"

"We learn to live with anything. We learn to live first of all with mortality. In any form, it is unacceptable, outrageous. Is it not? At this particular time you must have some thoughts on the subject. But let that pass. After the first realization that we are all going to die, that each of us is finite, is mortal, then there comes a series of questions. And nobody answers them. There are no answers, perhaps because the questions are too difficult to face. We ignore them. We turn away, as if they had never been raised in the first place. But they have, they have. And they cry out for answers."

"And your answers have been for quality rather than duration? Something like that?"

"I shouldn't even be that definite. I allow that some answer of that kind is logically possible, and that any man or woman has a right to make that answer. And that, as a physician, I can in good conscience go along with such an answer, help in working out its terms medically, physically. We are not gods, we doctors. At the best, we are helpers, with our skills at the disposal of the public. At the worst, we are meddlers. As you have become, I'm afraid."

"I can understand your resentment. But you ought to understand mine. You shouldn't have sent Elfinstone to break into my office. I resented that."

"Apparently."

"It was another error in judgment?"

"All right, I'll admit to that. As if it mattered. Yes, it was an error. Not to break in, but to use him. The fool! Garbage!"

"What have you done with him? Is he dead?"

"No. Not worth killing."

"He knows rather a lot."

"He isn't going to say anything. And if he did, no one would believe him."

"Why not?"

"A paranoid? A nut?"

"I don't understand . . ."

"No? I had him committed this afternoon. For observation. He's at Lindeman. Isn't that nice? Neat? What is he going to say? To whom? And with what effect?"

"What will happen to him?"

"Do you really care?"

"Don't you? He was your patient."

"I helped him for a while. And he survived for longer than he would have managed without me. He is beyond my help now . . ."

"But not beyond mine. There is still something left of the man."

"Something interesting? Something worth bothering with?"

"Isn't every human being worth bothering with?"

"No."

"I see," I said. I could not make him angry. But neither could I retreat so far as to bore him. "If you could make me believe that, then I could agree with you about . . . about everything. About what you've done with all those people."

"It would take too long. We haven't the time. It would change nothing. There are no choices."

"Aren't there?"

"I'm afraid not," he said.

The hand with the gun moved slightly, as though he had very nearly forgot that he was holding it and now had remembered.

"There are a couple of things, then, that I ought to tell you," I said.

"All right, but briefly."

"I'll be brief. For one thing, I've been talking with a Mr. Goodman in the district attorney's office. He knows everything I know about you, and about Swett and Curran. He will be seeing you tomorrow."

"I see. And the other thing?"

"It's related. It's simply that you won't be able to get away with this. There are too many people who know what I've been doing, and who know what I've discovered about you. If I were killed, there would be suspicion that would immediately turn to you."

"I quite agree. There would be suspicion. But suspicion is not conviction. And there would be no way to prove anything. A coincidence, that's all."

"That seems unrealistic," I said, using a professional tone.

"Does it? I am touched by your concern for me. But I have an alibi. I am with another patient."

"Who will lie for you?"

"Who depends upon me. As many of my patients do," he said, smiling with a self-congratulation that was even more hateful than the gun in his hand.

"But you will be changing that relationship, won't you?"

144

"No."

"You will. It will be a mutual dependence. An equality. Admit equality and Nietzsche starts to collapse."

"Very neat. Very nice. I admire that. Another woman might not be so smart in a situation like this. I regret this . . ."

"You will regret it more, afterwards. You will lose everything."

"And if I were to put this away," he said, moving the gun again, "and walk out of here, I still lose everything. So I have nothing to lose, do I? Either way it's bad. I have to pick, if you'll pardon the expression, my shot."

"It's a choice of how much you want to lose, then, isn't it?"

"What choice? Either way, I go to jail, don't I? But this way, I get to stay out unless they can prove I was here, which they won't. I . . . I shouldn't have started this conversation."

"But you did. You knew I am a psychiatrist. You wanted to play with me, to risk a little, to let me try to talk you out of shooting me. It wouldn't have been sporting the other way. Something like that?"

"Something like, yes."

"So, you see, there is a part of you that wants to be talked out of shooting me. That wants not to do it."

"Of course. I am not a butcher."

"No, you aren't. But how will you think of yourself if you do this?"

"I will have to live with that."

"As you have lived with killing Swett?"

"That was less complicated. He was of less value than you are. By the time he died, anyway, he was of less value. And I had to do that in order to save my other patients, in order to continue their treatments, in order to allow them to continue the lives they had chosen. That was not so hard to live with. He was in the way."

"As I am?"

"Yes."

"As your alibi will be. Sooner or later your other patient will come to understand what it was that you needed the alibi for. And will get in the way. And then you will have to do this again. And sooner or later you will become that butcher."

"We do what we must."

"You are denying responsibility. And choice. It's not like you."

"Enough of this."

"I bore you?"

"No. I cannot afford to listen any more. I know what I have to do.

It is as plain as a mathematical theorem, and there is no room for error . . ."

It wasn't working. I had not supposed that it would, but I could see that we were coming to a crisis, and that he was working himself up to pulling the trigger. Which meant that my choices were becoming clearer and increasingly immediate. I could either stand there like a target, like a turkey in a turkey shoot, and let him blast away at me. Or I could try to do something. My hope was that as a physician, he was not so comfortable with firearms as he had been with a hypodermic syringe, that the planning had been better than the execution would be, that he might, even at close range, miss . . .

My judo? Ridiculous! It was not a classroom situation, and I thought of what position I should try to assume, where to put my feet, what move to make, followed by what other move. I could imagine an exercise on a mat, but this was a real gun, and my body would not do any of those things, would not go leaping and posturing into extinction. I should have practiced more! Too late for that, though.

Still, my chances would be better if I were moving. But in what direction? Did it make any difference? The point was speed and surprise. Do it the way they do in the movies. Of course, in the movies, Randolph Scott would come bounding in to save the heroine . . . Or she would bluff the villain by calling out to him. To whom? I couldn't remember a name. But why not?

"Randy! He's got a gun!"

Very loud, as if he were behind Harney. And yes, dumb as it was, it worked, just for a fraction of a second, as Harney turned his head a little, and I ducked down behind the kitchen table and took a quick step to the left. The gun went off, but Harney had shot upwards, into the ceiling. It was terribly loud. Much louder than in the movies. I was angry at how loud it was, and I grabbed a large ceramic ashtray from the table and flung it at his head, and of course I missed. And he shot again and missed, and I guessed there were four more shots—there are supposed to be six shots, aren't there?—and threw a bowl. Noisy! The bullets and the shattering of the bowl . . .

"Get help!" I called, as if to someone.

It didn't even occur to me that he'd look around again, but he did, and this time I picked up the small step stool and hurled it at him, and he saw it coming and leapt out of the way, and the stool missed him, but he came down the wrong way and the gun went off and suddenly he was lying there on the floor and he'd shot himself in the foot.

I took a step toward him, then realized that he still had the gun in his hand and took another three steps back and hid behind the refrigerator.

"I'm shot," he said.

"I know."

"Help me."

"Throw out the gun. Throw it into the middle of the room."

"It'll go off."

"Put the safety on and then throw it out."

"Oh. Okay. It hurts. My foot, I mean. Not the safety."

I didn't answer.

"You didn't think that was funny? I thought it was funny."

He was trying to ingratiate himself, trying to make me laugh, trying to find a way around the situation.

"Throw the gun out. There isn't any choice any more. And there's no point in killing me if you can't get away with it, is there?"

"No, I guess not."

"Then throw it."

"Let's make a deal."

"What deal?"

"No prison. You won't bring charges."

"Throw the gun."

"I don't want to go to prison."

"You'll give me the names of all your patients. They will need help. All of them. The gun and the names, and I'll agree."

"Fuck you!" he said.

But then he threw the gun into the middle of the room. I got out from behind the refrigerator and picked it up. Felicity appeared, inspected the scene, arched her back in disapproval, and then withdrew. I went to get water and dishtowels so that I could take a look at the foot where he'd shot himself.

Seven

Martin arrived just before the police left. I'd bandaged Dr. Harney's foot and then called the police, and they'd come and had taken him to Cambridge City Hospital. And a detective had talked to me for a half-hour, and I'd told him more or less what had happened that evening and why it had happened. I didn't mention Ted Goodman. Goodman had tried to help, and I'd need his help again.

Martin thought I was crazy. I agreed with him. There was the broken ashtray on the floor, and the smashed bowl, and it looked as though a lunatic had been storming around in the room. It even smelled crazy. That was the cordite or whatever they put in the bullets. That smell lasted a long while. Even the next day I thought I could smell it.

Martin was very quiet. He was torn between sympathy—after all, I'd been shot at—and rage. Why hadn't I listened to him? Didn't I see that his advice had been right, now that it had come to this?

No, I didn't see it. I saw it, of course, but in fact, the way things had worked out had been all right. I'd paid off Adam Swett for the inadequacies of my attention when he had come to me. I had paid Harney back for putting Elfinstone up to breaking into my apartment.

"What about Elfinstone?" Martin asked.

I told him that Elfinstone was safe for the night, that Harney had put him in Lindeman.

"You going to take him on?" Martin asked.

"No, I don't think so. I'll turn him over to someone else. I think it would be better that way. For him."

And that was what I did. Elfinstone went to see a colleague, and he may work out some of his problems. It was odd, really, because he had been the one who had burgled my office, the one at whom I had felt the original rush of anger that had started me off on the whole project. And he had crumpled at the end, going to see Dr. Harney, as he had promised to do, and then, with the weird feeling that Harney could read his mind, knew what he was thinking, and could somehow see his intention of going to meet me at the clinic as if it had been imprinted in red letters on his forehead, had told Harney about my second visit, my promises, my threats . . .

But I couldn't blame him. I could be displeased, in the way one is always displeased by the regression of a patient. But that was the nature of his condition. And I arranged for treatment, not by me. He had too many associations, too many kinds of guilt and anger that were associated with me. I don't think I was similarly burdened. I understood that he had merely been Harney's instrument.

Harney is not using his instruments any more. He is under observation at Bridgewater, going through a ninety-day stay during which time his lawyers and the district attorney's office work out the plea bargaining. If he will plead guilty to felonious assault (an assault on me), then there will be a suspended sentence. But the felony conviction will lose him his license to practice medicine. And I will have kept my bargain with him. About which I feel quite scrupulous.

I called on Helene Purvis, telling her what Adam Swett had been trying to do, that he had not betrayed her or any of the plans they had made together. I think she believed me. She deserves a better chance than she had been giving herself. There was more I should have liked to do for her, but nothing I could do. Not unless she asked. And even her asking would be a great step forward. Anyway, a start . . .

I also went to see Lila Swett. I put that off for a while, not liking the woman. But I was wrong, had been wrong all along. She had known all the time.

"But how would it have looked?" she asked. "All his life he worked to get where he was, and then the strain of it turned him into another person. I knew about Helene, and I knew about Dr. Harney. And I knew about Adam's plans . . . But I also knew how it would have looked. The first black dean at Harvard, and what does he do? Shacks up with some woman? Goes on speed? We can't afford it! I'm proud, Dr. Chayse, and maybe that's a sin. But I'm not proud for myself. I'm proud for my people. And I didn't want to add any to the burden that's already there. So I kept my mouth shut. And I was angry when you came around, stirring things up . . . Angry and afraid. But I'm not, now."

"I'm glad I came to see you," I said.

"I'm glad you came. Maybe now I can remember Adam a little, and grieve for him. He wasn't a bad man, you know."

"I never thought so."

What else? I wrote a long letter to John to explain what had happened. But then I put it in a drawer to think about for a while. I haven't mailed it. That's over, somehow.

Martin is not over. He is convinced that I'm crazy. I keep telling him that crazy is his word for different, and that we are, indeed, different. But that we can still get along. I have to learn to be a little less prickly, a little less defensive. Martin has to learn how to hold without clutching. But there's hope.

Clare Brinton died today. I shall go to her funeral in New York. It is an occasion of great sadness for me, for I have lost a friend and a mentor. But I am looking forward to the chance to think. About her, and about myself in ways that she taught me to do. The question I have to ask, I suppose, is how I feel about what I did.

Certainly, there were satisfactions in it. And the results were acceptable and better than acceptable. But it would be a mistake to suppose that from such motives and through such behavior, there is any necessity of reaching these kinds of results. It is important not to learn the wrong lessons from experience . . . which is blank until we interpret it. It was exhilarating to snoop around and to meddle in the lives of these people. But it was also dangerous, for them as well as for myself. Mysteries are usually more complicated than Elfinstone's paperback thrillers let on. There are lives out there, each of them delicately balanced and fragile, vulnerable to shock. As I am, myself.

So, in the end, I may have learned a kind of diffidence from all this brashness and boldness. That was, perhaps, what Clare Brinton was trying to tell me. And maybe what Martin was trying to tell me, too.

But none of us can ever hear such things until we are ready to listen. And often that's too late.

There is a lock on my files now.

And I have bought that cloisonné pot.

About the Author

LYNN MEYER is Director of Research for Social Change, Inc., a non-profit organization she founded for funding and supporting women in academic research. She reads—and now writes—mysteries as a hobby. She was born in New York and took her B.A. degree at Vassar College. She lives in Cambridge, Massachusetts, and has three children. This is her first novel.